ONE WOMAN'S STORY:

AND *THEN THERE WERE TWELVE*

KATE HERRIOTT

outskirts
press

Outskirts Press, Inc.
http://www.outskirtspress.com

ISBN: 978-1-9772-0432-5

ONE WOMAN'S STORY:
AND THEN THERE WERE TWELVE

Monday morning raised its head beautifully. The sun was out and the day held the promise of a lovely autumn with gold and red leaves dotting the landscape; however, I hardly noticed. I was in such a hurry to drive downtown and to find a parking space in one of the two available lots where jurors were allowed to park that I arrived naked for jury duty. Embarrassing, you say? You immediately thought that this was a dream sequence, didn't you? Sad to say it was real. Okay, I wasn't literally naked. I had forgotten my earrings, and I dare any of you who have pierced ears to tell me you don't feel naked going out in public without your earring of choice for the day. I knew people were staring at me and thinking, "She might look good if she had only accessorized."

I felt like hiding in a corner. Snubbed. I was also frustrated because I obviously had not yet learned to carry an extra pair of earrings in my purse.

There were people from every walk of life on jury-picking day. I called it jury picking. It was like someone pulled all the apples off the tree, put them into one large basket or vat, and then culled out by some means the ones they did not want. "That apple isn't the right color or that apple is misshapen. Or even, she didn't remember her earrings, so how could she remember the evidentiary testimony needed if she was selected for a jury?" We were thrown back into the huge vat to be sorted again to simply wait until the end of the day or to be sent to another judge's courtroom to see if we were good enough for that trial. And so it went. It was almost a form of profiling. According to the *Oxford Dictionary*, "Profiling: the recording and analysis of a person's psychological and behavioral characteristics, so as to assess or predict their capabilities in a certain sphere or to assist in identifying a particular subgroup of people." Yes, that sounded like jury picking to me.

In some states jury picking lasted only one day. If one wasn't picked for a jury, that was it. One and done. In other states one had two whole weeks to be picked for a jury and could even serve on more than one jury during that time period. In my state, I was thankful that it was one day, which meant if I wasn't picked, I didn't have to go back. I didn't like being rejected and sent back to the vat, but then I wasn't sure that I was ready to be responsible for someone else's life. It seemed enough to be responsible for my own life and those of my three dogs, Hopeful, Joyful, and Perky, as well as my grouchy cat, Skinny.

After being rejected in the first courtroom I had been sent to, I and the others rejected were sent back to the original room where everyone had first met. There we found people who had not been called at all as well as others who had been called and then rejected from courtrooms other than ours. People were reading books or looking at their phones, and some had their computers and were fast at work. Other people were even trying to sleep. I couldn't decide what I wanted to do, so I simply watched people for a while. I didn't try to talk to anyone; that's not what we true introverts usually do. I looked out of the row of windows, and could see the sun was out and from the movement of the bushes, there appeared to be a gentle breeze. I observed that it was a little courtyard. I knew that was where I wanted to be. I left my chair and went up to the clerk behind a counter, who was still working in our room. "May I go out to the courtyard?" I asked.

"Sure," he said, "just give me your name and juror number, so that I know where you are if it turns out that we call you for another jury."

I complied and went out into the courtyard. Once there I walked around for a while and then sat on one of the benches that were provided. Some people were eating out there. Others were reading either a newspaper or a book. I had neither, so I decided to check my text messages. There were a few to read and respond to.

I heard a couple of people in the courtyard talking about what they would do if their names were called for a jury. Big talk. They were discussing the farcical answers they wanted to give to questions from the attorneys. One of the men said, "I'll tell the attorney and even the judge that I don't have to answer their stupid questions." These people were full of bravado. I wondered if the time came and they were called to be on a jury whether or not they would stick to what they were saying. I kind of doubted it. People were funny.

A woman was speaking on her phone. It sounded like she was talking to a lover or spouse and things weren't going well for her. He or she evidently had a lot to say to her and must have been placing her on the defensive. Every so often she would get out, "But honey..."

After about thirty minutes of enjoying my time in the outdoors, a woman came to the courtyard door and called my name. She said that my name and number were called to go to yet another courtroom. I was called as juror number five and had to stand fifth in line while the rest of the prospective jurors were called which took approximately twenty minutes. As we walked into the courtroom, those of us first in line were directed to sit in the jury seats. It was going to be a criminal trial, I was sure, since a vast number of people had been called to line up as possible jury members for this courtroom. Every seat in the entire room was filled. From the little research that I had performed, I thought I knew what the attorneys looked for when they questioned prospective jurors and who they preferred not to have on a jury. I had answered everything truthfully on the questionnaire, which we had completed earlier, and did not believe that a lawyer would want me; thus I wasn't too concerned.

The attorneys each told stories and asked questions. I answered a hypothetical football question the prosecutor asked me. I had always been good at hypothetical thinking, but I didn't know if I had answered the question the way the prosecutor wanted. There must have been a hidden meaning in there, I thought. In some odd way, about three hours after being called to line up for the courtroom, when the culling process was over, I was still sitting in a jury seat. I was one of the chosen, empty earlobes and all. How did that happen? We had to stand, raise our hands, and be formally sworn in as jurors.

The judge, the prosecutor and the defense lawyer all shared legal knowledge with us about what was expected. They each made it clear that the defendant was presumed innocent unless the prosecution proved its case against him. I listened carefully to each word they said. After all, I was now a chosen person, even if partially naked. I felt the responsibility lying quite heavily on my narrow shoulders. I knew that the defendant wouldn't be the only one praying for the correct verdict. I would be praying every day, not wanting to make a mistake where his life was concerned.

I had been known for making mistakes in my life that either had affected or could have greatly affected me, even as an adult. In looking back I remembered a big one as a child. I was walking on a railroad track when I heard a train coming. (No, my parents did not know that I was doing such a thing.) I couldn't jump off to the side because I was up on the railroad bridge. I had to climb down on the bridge trestle and hang on to the side of the trestle until the train went by overhead. I could also say that I never did that again. I had made mistakes, but I usually learned from them. I did not want to make a mistake that would affect whether or not someone went to jail.

The judge explained to us, the jury, the nature of the trial and the charges against the defendant. The defendant was a medical doctor in our city who was charged with over-prescribing pain medication to his mostly geriatric patients. The exact charge was illegally dispensing a controlled substance. This case reminded me of a Florida doctor convicted a few years earlier of similar charges. I read about the case at that time. I thought he had prescribed around 20,000 pills of a pain medication to one person in ten months. That would have been sixty-six pills a day. Yes, something sounded wrong about that, but our case would stand on its own. It would be the duty of our jury (twelve jury members and one alternate) to decide if the charges had been proven by the prosecution.

I did not remember seeing any news about this doctor's arrest. Perhaps the news media had not found it interesting enough, or perhaps something more salacious was going on at the time and reporters were sharing that particular news with the people. I used to be a news junkie and had news on television or radio almost constantly. I finally tired of hearing the same thing discussed over and over, day and night. In addition, the newscasters repeatedly shared their opinions and not just facts. I wanted facts. I could establish my own opinions, so unless it was necessary, I just checked my Twitter feed once or twice a day where I followed two news outlets, one local and one national. I could keep up with most of what was going on without getting bogged down with so much negativity.

I had heard from my neighbor Florence that jurors in past years were not allowed to take notes. Not only did they allow us to take notes, but they also gave us binders with jury information in them and pads of paper to write on. The judge also informed us that we would be given an opportunity after each witness to write out any question we had for the witness. The question would be delivered to the judge. The judge would then meet with the two attorneys, and he would determine whether or not the question could be asked. I thought this idea was great.

The attorneys began their opening statements. Since this court had begun later in the day, after opening statements, the judge called an adjournment for the day. We were told to be back at 8:30 the next morning to continue. I had to admit that I was thankful that this trial did not contain a murder or have something to do with young children. To my way of thinking, such things would have made being a juror much more stressful.

I was Harri Bedlington, or otherwise known in the courthouse as the naked-ear lady. I had my own charming little florist shop in the go-to area of our city. My shop was called Creations by Harri, and I had been in business on my own for about seven months. Before that, during and after college I worked for Rodney at his florist shop called Le Fluer. I knew it was misspelled French, but that was Rodney. It wouldn't have been very difficult to have corrected the error after I shared with him the correct spelling, but he wouldn't be deterred. He said since he had done well with his business with it misspelled, he would keep it that way. He was superstitious about changing it, as he was superstitious about many things. He had horseshoes tacked up on walls in a couple of places in his shop. There were also no mirrors in Le Fluer, because of the superstition that looking into a mirror could steal one's soul. That was Rodney; however, we became good friends when we worked together.

I had two brothers, William and Oliver, who were the bane of my existence for years. They were either getting into trouble or doing their best to get me into trouble. In the last few months they had discovered females, each a female, to be exact, and they appeared to have calmed down some. These were the first women they had dated since their few stabs at it in high school, and my brothers were decidedly out of their teens. They worked hard to keep me away from the women. I thought it was because they were afraid I might share some of their outrageous shenanigans. After the years I put up with them, It would have served them right.

My brothers did everything together. They worked at the same company. They had the same friends. They double dated. They even lived together in the house they bought from our parents. My concern was that if they ever married, they would just move their wives into the same bedrooms they had lived in for the majority of their lives. I already felt a deep sympathy for any future wives of my brothers.

I received a jury summons when I had only been in business for two months. I was thankful I had been able to put it off for a few months until things were running smoothly and I was sure that I could be absent without losing my business. There was a person who originally had said he would help me by working with my assistant, Adelyn, while I responsibly carried out my civic duty; however, before the time came for jury duty, the man was arrested. His trial was set for next August where he would be tried for his crimes. He was sure to receive a guilty verdict, and be placed on death row at the New Mesa Centennial (NMC, also called in our state No More Chances) Penitentiary. Go figure. That was a whole other story.

As it turned out, my friend Darla, with whom I had worked at Le Fluer, had an abundance of vacation days she had built up working for Rodney. Recently Rodney informed

Darla that she had to start using her vacation days or she would begin losing them. She had therefore taken days off from Le Fluer and worked with Adelyn in my shop while I was on jury duty. She had Rodney's approval, of course. Darla's husband was a fire investigator, and they hardly ever had time for vacations. When I asked her to help, Darla said to me in her southern twang, "Sweetie, friends share their fried green tomatoes" (an example of what I call Darla-isms). I took it to mean she wanted to help me out. What a great friend, which reminded me of a quote: "Friendship is born at that moment when one person says to another, What! You too? I thought I was the only one." I imagined everyone could relate to that quotation by C. S. Lewis.

As jurors we were instructed by the judge that we were not to look up anything about the case we were to hear. I fully understood that; however, I wondered if it also meant that we could not look up information as to what was a normal amount of pain medication, if there was a normal amount. Thinking about it further, I decided that it probably meant that we were to know only what was presented to us in court for making our decisions. Okay, I decided I could refrain from internet searches that could in any way have anything to do with the case, much as I wanted to search out some answers. Two years earlier, before I had gone through my life-altering crisis, I probably would have just gone ahead, thinking I had the right to do so. I was a rather silly and obstinate person back then. That silliness and obstinacy still creeped out of me every once in a while, I was sorry to say.

At 8:30 Tuesday morning the jury was found sitting around a large table in the jury room. Some of the jurors were chatting with each other. Some jurors were reading. Other jurors were looking at their phones, but all were sitting by that time. The woman sitting next to me on the right said, "I like your earrings."

I knew it. I knew she had been looking at me strangely the day before. I responded, "Thank you. I forgot my earrings yesterday. I felt so naked."

The woman looked at me, smiled, and lied by saying, "Oh, I hadn't noticed." Of course she had noticed. Every time she spoke to me the day before she would look at me directly and then turn her eyes toward one of my ears. Every time.

We received word to line up and go into the courtroom. We had specific seats so that the judge and the attorneys knew the names of each juror by our seat; thus we entered the courtroom in numerical order. I assumed it kept us from stepping on or tripping all over each other in the courtroom trying to get to our assigned seats. I supposed that could be disconcerting to the order of the court.

The prosecutor began interviewing witnesses. Evidently he had quite a few witnesses lined up to talk to about receiving medication. I knew these were days that I had to persevere to keep my focus on what was being said and not let my mind get whisked away to idea-land with some outlandish thoughts brought on by a single word I might hear. Does your mind do that, too? We had a short break around 10:15 and were back in the courtroom by 10:30.

Not too long after we were seated and the next witness had been called and taken the stand, the man in the chair in front of me began shaking all over and then fell out of his chair onto the floor. The judge told the bailiff to call 911. The juror continued shaking for a period of time, and pandemonium reigned in the courtroom. The man then fell quiet, without any movement.

The judge told the jury to leave the courtroom and return to the jury room, and he asked for the courtroom to be cleared. You should have heard the decibel level in the jury room. You likely would have put your fingers over your ears to tone down the sound. It appeared as though everyone of us was talking at once and loudly. We had all experienced a shock, for sure. At 11:00 we were told that we were excused to go to lunch but to be back in the jury room before 1:30. The bailiff evaded, with aplomb, the questions that were tossed at him about our missing juror.

With such an extended time for lunch, I decided to find a place to eat outside of the courthouse, even though there was a small café in the basement. I thought about the juror who had the seizure and was curious as to what happened. Perhaps the stress of being on a jury had brought on the seizure. I had already prayed about the man but wondered what else could be done. Had his family been informed? Surely he had been taken to the hospital. There had been very little time to learn much about him, even though he had been one of the more vociferous of the group. I recalled that I heard him say that he taught art in a public school.

I knew next to nothing about the different kinds of seizures. I remembered as a child sitting on the front steps of my house, and at times our neighbor's boy would come over to sit with me. Sometimes he would have a seizure. None of us children found anything unusual about it. It was just what he did. Thankful for my iPhone, I looked up seizures. According to the Mayo Clinic, there were six types of generalized seizures and all sorts of risk factors that could cause them.

It was still a beautiful day to be outdoors. After eating I just wandered around a bit, looking in store windows. Keeping track of time, at 1:10 I headed back toward the courthouse. As each person filtered into the jury room, more and more talk took place about our missing juror. The woman who had been sitting beside him to his left ostensibly knew his name. She said that she had called the hospitals during our lunchtime trying to get some information, but none had been offered to her. Someone ventured that "Usually people with seizures get up fine after a seizure and just continue on." We did not know if he would be back or if we would continue, except with our alternate. Maybe the affected juror was simply resting up in another room until time for us to go back to the courtroom. Everything was presumptive at the moment.

While much chatting was taking place, we received our call to line up and head back into the courtroom. After we were seated, we noticed that the courtroom was empty except for the judge, the lawyers, and the defendant. The judge spoke to us saying, "Your fellow juror, number ten, Mr. George, died this morning after his seizure."

The audible intake of breath from twelve people made an exceptional sound in the room. The judge continued, "What I need to know now is this: because of the tragedy, are there any sitting on this jury who feel that they cannot continue as a juror in this trial? If so, please raise your hand." After about thirty to forty-five seconds he declared, "No one raised his or her hand, so we will continue with the trial. Juror number thirteen, you are now the twelfth juror and will be considered juror ten. Please move over into the seat vacated by juror ten. Bailiff, you may open the doors to the courtroom."

I remembered that the Mayo Clinic site had mentioned something called SUDEP, sudden unexpected death in epilepsy. That must be what had happened. How sad! That was the first death I had ever witnessed, and I was surely hopeful that it would be the last. No one expects to be on a jury and have one of the jurors die in front of them. I thought the odds of that happening must be tremendous, although I was sure that it had happened at some time. This Mr. George had looked relatively young and in good shape, too, but from what I read I realized that seizures could hit at any age. It was a lot for me to take in.

I didn't have more time to reflect on the tragedy, as the prosecutor continued with prosecution witnesses the entire afternoon. I was trying to discern from the witnesses whether or not they had received too many opioids, unnecessary opioids, a higher-than-necessary milligram dosage, or if the doctor was making additional money from the prescriptions. The prosecutor finished with his last witness at 5:45, and the attorney for the defense had only about four questions for that witness, so we were dismissed at 6:00.

After arriving home and feeding the dogs, I took them for a long walk. They loved our walks, and the walk helped clear my head from everything that had happened that day. My three rescued dogs were quite different from each other. The Doberman was sweet, funny, and needy. The Redbone Coonhound was a bull in a china shop and would follow her nose anywhere. If she ever got loose she would keep following her nose and never return. She made me laugh, though. My Plott Hound was a sweet and precious dog. You would not know from her that the Plott Hound was bred to hunt bear.

When we returned from our walk, I turned on the television to keep my mind busy while I fixed my dinner. My attention got riveted to the television when I heard the name of John George. I sat down to watch. The news crew talked about how he had died in the courtroom. They interviewed two of the people who had been in the courtroom at the time of the seizure. They both seemed to enjoy getting their minute of fame on television. They definitely exaggerated everything that happened. They had John George standing and yelling before falling. They said that he fell onto the woman sitting next to him and she had shoved him onto the floor. None of that had happened. The way they delivered their stories sounded as if they had been coached about what to say. Evidently the truth had been too boring for television.

The newscaster also said that there would be an autopsy to more fully determine the cause of Mr. George's demise, because his parents and siblings said they had not known him to have a seizure before. The newscaster continued by saying that when asked about seizures, "Mr. George's lovely wife told me, 'I've seen John have a seizure twice from taking drugs. He had wanted to keep the information from his family about using drugs and the seizures'."

From what I had read a seizure could happen at any time to anyone; however, I understood the family's need to be sure.

I called Adelyn to see how things were going at Creations by Harri. She said, "Great. I'm ever so thankful to have Darla working with me. She sure knows what she is doing, and she's a hoot, to boot." She continued, "Julie was a lifesaver, as we actually had tour buses in our neighborhood today."

Julie was my latest hire, and she worked the majority of her part-time hours in the front part of the shop while Adelyn and I worked in the back making floral arrangements.

"I have to go back tomorrow, Adelyn," I disclosed. "In fact we may not be done until Thursday or Friday, from the way it looks right now."

"That's okay. Truly, we're doing fine," Adelyn said. "The good news is that we do not have any big events this weekend. Your being able to put off jury duty until we were past the wedding crush time was really a stroke of luck."

I had just finished speaking with Adelyn when my phone

rang. It was Bolen. Isaiah Bolen was a detective with the police department in our city. We had gone from being adversaries when we first knew each other to being friends. We were taking that friendship nice and slow.

"How'd your day go, Harri?" he asked. "Did you hear about the man who died in one of the courtrooms? I imagine that was the talk of the courthouse today."

"Bolen, it was my courtroom. That man, John George, was in the chair right in front of me when it happened, when he died," I answered. "I had a front-row seat and I couldn't help but wish I had been seated far away, like in the top row of a balcony."

"I'm so sorry. How awful for you," Bolen commented. He continued, "Just in case something arises, why don't you write down the details you remember about the episode? Then, if for some reason the death turns out to be a suspicious one, you needn't be concerned about not remembering those details. We'll know more about it after we receive the autopsy report. It most likely was an accidental or natural death, but we never can tell."

"It surely had to be the result of the seizure. I mean, he had been with us all morning, and he had talked and laughed and appeared to be quite well. That was the first person I've seen die, so I suppose I wouldn't know natural versus unnatural," I declared, "however, I will sit down as soon as we quit speaking and write up what I remember about this morning. It might actually prove to be a cathartic act."

We said goodbye. I went in to my bedroom and turned on my computer and began typing what I remembered offhand about the morning. I wrote, "I'm writing what I remember about John George before he died. We, that is we the jury, were in the jury room during our 10:15 break on Tuesday. Our Mr. George had been talking fairly loudly with the two people who sat directly to his right. Did I catch any of it? I think it had something to do with the gullibility of today's students. Yes, he said that they were so used to their helicopter parents hovering over everything they did that they couldn't make decisions that were well thought out. They just followed the crowd. He said it was easy to dupe them and he often enjoyed doing that. I think he stayed in his seat while he was talking. He also drank from a Yeti cup that he had brought with him. I didn't know if he had filled it at home or if he had filled it with coffee or water from the jury room. Of course he could have purchased a drink from somewhere along the way. I wondered if his Yeti cup was still on the table in the jury room. He did use the restroom after that, because he was still in there when we were lining up to go back into the courtroom. He high-fived the man who sat next to him when he came out of the restroom. I remembered that part because I was kind of a germaphobe and wondered if he had washed his hands. I didn't think we had been back inside the courtroom more than five minutes before I noticed the shaking begin. He shook in his chair for about thirty seconds and then fell out of the chair onto the floor. He must have continued shaking for at least one and one-half minutes to two minutes longer. Then he was just lying there without any movement. At that point we were sent out of the courtroom."

After I finished, I turned off my computer and went into my great room to relax and think about the court case. As a juror, I needed to consider the trial. If I were old and in a lot of pain or even aware that I was dying I might not want to go the regular morphine route often used in hospice care. That could leave me groggy and not aware of various aspects in my life, so I thought I might want something less potent, perhaps an opioid pill. I would want to live my last months or days with as clear a mind as I could. That is what I would want. In deliberating this case, I could not go on my feelings. I had to go by the law and the evidence.

What exactly was the law about dispensing opioids? One witness said that the CDC guidelines indicated that physicians could dispense the needed opioids to cancer and hospice patients. I thought I also remembered someone testifying that those drugs could be given to surgical patients for a limited time. Okay. So far it appeared that was mostly what that doctor had done. The CDC also urged doctors to avoid opioid prescriptions for patients with chronic pain, but according to the witnesses that we heard from, there were people in severe pain who were being undertreated. It appeared that it was difficult for a doctor to stay balanced between guidelines and laws and correctly treating patients under those circumstances. We were told that some physicians were so afraid of losing their licenses to practice medicine that they would not provide an opioid prescription to any patient.

According to a witness testimony, my state had policies in place that were updated that year. Any new changes to the previous policies did not affect the case I was sitting on. My case was to follow the policies created four years earlier, as those were the policies in place for the time the defendant was charged. The policies appeared to be mostly guidelines for the physicians to bear in mind but from what I heard in court, physicians were expected to follow them fairly closely.

I considered, if I took six pills (one every four hours) in twenty-four hours for ten days, that would be sixty pills, so I thought anything over that could be considered excessive, unless the prescription said to take two pills every four hours. That would be 120 pills in ten days, which would be 3,600 pills in ten months. I supposed some people might need that. For chronic pain, not associated with surgery or cancer, that number of pills might be considered excessive. But, what did I know about it? Then, too, it could also depend on the strength of the pill. Or it could depend on the severity of a person's pain. The guidelines did recommend using lower strengths when prescribing opioids. I sure wished we had a chart of some kind to help with this issue. Of course I supposed every patient was different too, which would affect the dose given. This matter wasn't easy for us, the patients, or the physicians.

Wednesday morning I was up and feeling somewhat refreshed after a fairly good night's sleep. It was shocking even to me that I slept as well as I did having watched someone die during the day. I wondered how the rest of the jury slept. Was I cold hearted? I hoped not. Who likes to think of themselves in that way? Maybe such a stressful day just made my body and mind need sleep. I preferred that concept.

Checking my phone for the day's news, I didn't see anything about John George. I hoped that was a good omen. I was truly sorry that John George had died. I unequivocally was. I was also sorry that I had been there to observe it. I hadn't seen anyone die before, but I had known people who had been killed. I really did not want another murder in my life. Was that thought selfish on my part? Probably. If I found out that he had been murdered, I knew I would want whoever had committed the murder to be caught and arrested. I knew me and that I would feel obligated to help see that outcome come to fruition—discovering the guilty party. I just preferred that he had died of natural causes, so to speak.

By 8:35 we jurors were almost all gathered in the jury room. Someone had to be late. We had been called to go into the courtroom, but we had to send word back to the judge that we were waiting for a late juror. Why was someone late for court? The man knew he had to go through security, and the line in the morning extended out the door and sometimes around the corner of the block.

He held up the entire court because he did not leave home on time. He walked in twelve minutes late, with excuses of course, about the long line downstairs. Who can do that? There should be a fine for that, I thought. Actually, once on a court case, jurors should have a door with a shortcut to security. Something for a suggestion box. We were, again, called to come into the courtroom.

It was encouraging that the prosecutor had only three witnesses left for us to hear. We hoped that meant by the afternoon the defense lawyer would offer the case for the defense.

One difficulty that day for the jury was that a couple of the female witnesses either did not speak into the microphone or were not speaking loudly enough, and we had to strain to hear them. Even when the judge told them to speak up, they still spoke in the same soft way. It was frustrating. If any people on the jury had their hearing lessened in any way and didn't want to ask again for the witness to speak up, they could have missed a portion of the testimony. My hearing was fine but I definitely strained to hear their testimony. The judge should probably have been more proactive in getting the witnesses to speak directly into the microphone or to speak louder. Something else for the theoretical suggestion box? I might just fill up an entire box myself.

I brought my lunch that day, since I was aware that we would have a shorter lunch period than we had on Tuesday. I wandered downstairs, found a table with chairs in a large hallway, and made myself at home. I looked at my phone for any texts I had received that morning, since I had to keep my phone turned off while in the courtroom. There were a few from friends wondering where I was. I had neglected to tell them that I was on jury duty. I answered their texts. I saw that I had received a text from Bolen. I gave him a quick call and was able to reach him. As we talked he communicated, "The autopsy of John George was completed. I can't share anything about it." He mentioned that the medical examiner would be sending off samples for toxicology tests. I was aware that toxicology tests were standard with autopsies; however, in this instance, since Bolen specifically mentioned it, I took it as a clue to the death. I felt sure it was considered a suspicious death.

I supposed that John George could have been being poisoned for a long time and it just hit him, but if that were the case, I thought he surely would have appeared sick in some way before the seizure. He seemed hale and hearty in the jury room. I was curious about what happened to him. As far as I knew, any poison that could cause a quick death would have been given to him at some point that morning. At any point that morning, say from 6:00 until 10:30. I'd planned to do some poison research when I arrived home that day to get an idea of what poisons acted precipitously fast.

We jury members all arrived back from lunch on time, but an expert witness wasn't expected for an extra fifteen minutes, which kept us in the jury room even longer. People were still talking about John George's death, and I understood why. It was rather a shock to all of us. I didn't share with them what I had deduced from Bolen. I mostly just listened. I did ask, "Did any of you know him before becoming a juror?" I looked and saw mostly negative head shakes. The person two chairs down on the right from where John George had sat was just staring straight ahead. Mr. Stare Guy noticed me looking at him, and he turned to look in the other direction. "What's that about?" I wondered.

Back in the courtroom the defense called witnesses the rest of the afternoon. What I had gathered earlier from the prosecution's expert witness was that 49,000 people in the United States had overdosed in the past year from opioid medications. In fact 72,000 died from drug overdoses in one year. That was big-time stuff. She also stated that physical therapy helped those with back pain more than taking opioids did. Interesting. The thing I wondered about: were those 49,000 people who had died from opioids, taking them legally or illegally? Surely they weren't all deaths from overprescribing. I sent that question to the judge as this expert witness's testimony drew to a close. The judge asked the question. The witness said that illicit street drugs, not prescription drugs, were now leading the abuse of opioids and those were coming from labs. She continued to tell us that many of those drugs were from labs in China and had come into the United States through the auspices of the Mexican drug cartels. I had not been aware of that fact. We were hearing some very interesting truths about drugs. In reality I had never used the term *opioid* before the trial.

I tried to remember if I had ever taken an opioid. Ah, yes, I thought I probably had. I didn't remember what it was, though. There was a chance that my mother remembered. It was my first year in college and I had my wisdom teeth extracted during Christmas vacation. Two of the teeth were under bones and the oral surgeon had to cut through the bone to dig out the teeth. I'm sure I was thankful at the time to have something to take the edge off the pain. I did remember having a fair amount of pain for a couple of days. When I came home from the surgery, Suzi-Q, our family dog, jumped up to see me, sniffed me, and then ignored me for a whole week until, evidently, I lost the blood smell or whatever it was that made her avoid me.

The defense expert agreed with much of what the prosecution expert had asserted. They also both agreed that it was often difficult for doctors to adhere to the "guidelines" when a patient was in obvious pain. Importantly, for the physicians, even though they were termed only guidelines, those guidelines, when taken to court in our country, had been used to convict at least one physician. An expert said that physicians needed to carefully document all reasons for prescribing opioids as well as document anything else they were doing for the patient to lessen the pain, such as prescribing pain therapies. Physicians were also advised to order urine tests to be sure a patient was not taking more medication than prescribed. One person said that the guidelines placed a physician between a rock and a hard place.

That evening my friend Amy and I had plans to go out to Detective Bolen's acreage to ride his horses. Amy and I were going to Colorado for our vacation the next June, and since we would be riding horses most of those days, we liked to get in practice time when we could. When Bolen's parents had moved to our area, they purchased property at the edge of the city that consisted of one hundred acres with two houses. Thanks to Bolen's parents, Amy and I were able to ride the horses on all one hundred acres. After Bolen decided to stay in the area, his parents sold him the second house and fifteen acres. According to Bolen, that second house required an enormous amount of work before it was habitable.

I would be saddling the horses myself that night, as Bolen was kept late at work. I was pleased that I could now do that task on my own. Bolen had made sure I could do it correctly. His horses had put up with my ineptness extremely well while I was learning. Bolen had rescued his three horses a couple of years earlier. They were beautiful, especially compared to pictures he showed to me of how they looked when he found them. I would never understand how people could mistreat their animals.

As we drove, Amy shared an update about her latest adventure, her doggy day care called Canine Sunset Vista. It was a ten-acre area with two intake buildings; one for the intake of large dogs, and the other for the intake of small dogs. She even had another building for a veterinarian who was coming to work on the property. She told me that the grand opening would be in two weeks. I was excited for her. She had spent the previous twelve years working as a legal secretary. The change would be awesome for her. I asked her how things were with her and Cian Bohannen, the man who had been her architect and head contractor for the whole project. They had become quite close and were seeing a lot of each other. She let me know that she considered everything between them wonderful. I was happy for her.

It was a beautiful evening for riding. The humidity had lowered, making it feel cooler than usual. I told Amy about being in the courtroom when John George died.

Amy said, "I went to high school with John. He was always quite a talkative one. He loved to gather and share any gossip he could. I haven't been around him since high school, so he may have changed."

I shared, "He seemed quite loquacious in the short time I was around him in the jury room."

Amy continued, "There was a girl in high school who followed him around like a puppy. She was a nice, rather attractive girl, but it was rather pathetic to watch her. He made over other girls all the time right in front of her. Her name was June Berghoff. I believe I heard she followed him to college and later married him. I guess he felt he needed to continue that puppy-like devotion he was used to from June by marrying her."

I disclosed, "I didn't interact with him at all, although I noticed others doing so. It was such a terrible shock, though, to see the seizure happening right in front of me, and then to find out that he had actually died after the seizure or from the seizure was heart wrenching. We had only seconds from the time we heard that he had died to deciding that we would stay with the jury. We were definitely still in a state of shock hearing of the death. I believe that was the reason, the shock, that no one raised a hand to indicate that they wouldn't stay with the jury. Now all of the jurors seem committed."

Amy conceded, "I cannot imagine how that must have affected each of you."

When I returned home, the dogs were not happy with me. Doubtless I still retained the smell of the horses on me. The girls previously had enjoyed going out to Bolen's acreage and getting to run free in the pasture. I didn't take them that night, since they were big dogs, and I didn't think Amy would enjoy being squashed in my car with three big dogs. I gave each of them a yak milk bone to make amends. Hopeful looked at me, then at her chew, and then looked at me, again, as if to say, "I'll forgive you this time. Just don't try it again."

Thursday morning came. I was hoping it would be the last day of the trial. I supposed it depended on four things: if the witness questioning was done in a timely manner, if the lawyer summations were not lengthy, if the judge's charge to the jury was brief, and if the jury could expeditiously agree on a verdict. Thinking about those four things I was not filled with confidence. It was not a slam dunk.

Checking the news, I saw that word was out about the George death being suspicious. I knew what the jury room talk would be about that day. Since that information was in the news, the other jurors probably knew as much about it as I did, although they might not know what was suspicious. Okay, I know you're thinking, "You don't know either," and I don't, for sure. I thought that I was on the right track, though.

I did some checking on poisons after I arrived home Wednesday evening. There were several poisons that I thought could be the source of Mr. George's death. I excluded a couple because they were too dangerous for the poisoner to handle. I needed more time for increased in-depth searching before I could hazard a guess as to the kind of poison that was used. Yes, my curiosity seemed to know no bounds. I knew that the lab reports would eventually tell what was used; however, I couldn't count on Bolen sharing that news with me. The bigger problem, then, would be to determine how it was administered and by whom.

I remembered what Amy had said about John George being a big gossip. I wondered if he was well known for that. Had he received some information that could harm someone's reputation, and that person had been made aware of it? Could John's gossiping have even turned into blackmail? All of this hypothesizing was getting me nowhere, as I hadn't the vaguest idea who the other person could be. Was it family? Was it a friend? Was it a drug dealer? Was it someone in the jury room? Who was it? Was it maybe even our defendant? Or what about the judge? Was that idea going a little too far? All I had at that point in time was questions. I had no answers.

I was right about one thing. The jurors were all in the jury room early, and the John George story was growing by the minute with all the talking and postulating. Mr. Stare Guy was raptly listening to everything that was being said. Well, so was I. Listening was a great tool for picking up ideas that could lead to paths to follow, but I talked as well. Mr. Stare Guy did not enter into any of the conversations.

One of the women, Sandra, who had sat to the left of John, said that John seemed a bit *handsy* (her word) around the women and maybe that was what had gotten him killed. She continued, "I had planned to report him later Tuesday for patting me on the rear. The last time he had leaned close to me the morning that he died, his breath had been terrible. I clued him in that he needed a breath mint."

Almost everyone laughed.

I asked her, "Did you give him one? A breath mint?"

Sandra answered back, "I wouldn't give him the time of day."

Well, so much for poor John. The people had gone from shock to sorrow and now to ridicule. The ridicule was continuing. There was also speculation as to how his death had been considered suspicious. Someone asked, "Sandra, did you decide to finish off old John instead of reporting him?"

Sandra hit her forehead with the palm of her hand and answered, "Why didn't I think of that?"

Finally we were called into the courtroom.

The first defense witness of the day was called. Before that witness, we had heard from two prosecution witnesses whose number of pills prescribed to them was iffy but not an obvious violation of the guidelines, from what I could tell. It also appeared that the doctor had not sold the medications at his office, so I deduced that he had not sold the medicine for profit. If he had sold medication from his office, the prosecutor had not shown us any evidence of it. Everything appeared to be prescriptions through a pharmacy. I couldn't help but be curious about whether or not a pharmacist had been involved and arrested too. I assumed pharmacists also had an obligation to comply with the guidelines. Again, my curiosity was at work. I wondered if it was strange that we hadn't seen a pharmacist as a witness. Did it mean the authorities had not seen fit to arrest a pharmacist? Or did it just mean they thought he or she would not be helpful to the case? And, here I caught myself speculating about the case when I knew I was only supposed to go by what we heard in the courtroom.

It came into my thoughts that a person could be guilty of a crime, but if the prosecution did not prove the case, the person could go free. Even if I believed a person to be guilty, I had to remember it had to be proven. I didn't think I had ever considered such an eventuality before then. That dilemma surely could cause a conflict within a juror. I wondered how many people were convicted because a juror felt the defendant was guilty even though the prosecution had not proved them guilty. Kind of scary, wasn't it?

I took my lunch again that day. As we broke for lunch I knew we still had at least one afternoon witness and the summations. It didn't look like the jury would be deliberating that day, not unless the judge had us stay late into the evening. I didn't know if the court system did that; had a jury stay late. I was beginning to realize that there was a lot in this world that I didn't know, and it would be wise to pick up every fragment of knowledge I could as I meandered through this life. Up until then I had not looked at most things in life as a chance learning experience, but rather as something to be lived through. I would try to make that change in the way I lived.

I checked my text messages. Bolen said, "I'd like to come by and take a statement from you about the death of John George. I'll call you later to see if you are home, and I'll swing by, if that works for you." He imparted that he would also be coming by the courthouse that afternoon. I assumed that the police needed to get the names of all of the jurors so that they could speak with them. They also would need to speak to anyone else who had been inside the courtroom who could have had any way of contacting a juror that morning of John George's death.

I wondered if the courtrooms were kept locked when not in use or if anyone could walk in and have access to the juror chairs. If so, it probably also meant that anyone would then have admittance through the door that led to the jury room, if it wasn't kept locked. That would give the opportunity for a multitude of people to have access to a juror.

I could foresee that the police contacting the jurors would cause a little hubbub among them. They might not know about it before leaving that day, unless they were notified during their midafternoon break or at the end of our jury day. I had hoped we would finish with the trial that day and John George's death would no longer be an issue of conversation among the jury members.

We were called into the courtroom for the afternoon

session. The defense called a witness. After the prosecutor questioned the witness, the lawyers had a sidebar with the judge. In this sidebar they met at the very front of the judge's platform to talk. The witness had not as yet been excused and was not supposed to be able to hear the lawyers and judge, but they were close enough to the witness that she may have picked up a few words. (That concerned me. I wondered if the judge had ever had that point tested. One more thing for the suggestion box.) The court reporter used headphones during the sidebar. Evidently the sound of the voices speaking into the microphone on the judge's bench went directly into the court reporter's headphones.

When the lawyers and judge finished speaking, the judge said to the court, "The defendant, although it is not incumbent on him to do so, will be taking the stand to testify. We will take our break now and then resume with the defendant when we return."

During the break my earring-noticing friend on my right talked about training her two small dogs. She had some funny stories to tell. It reminded me of taking Perkie to manners class. She was so distracted watching all of the people and the other dogs that the trainer came over and gave her a new name. She called her Ms. ADD (short for Attention Deficit Disorder). I had to laugh as I thought, like mother like daughter.

Back in the courtroom, as the lawyers were getting ready, I began to question why this case was not heard by a federal court instead of a district court. I didn't know why I hadn't thought about it before, but for some reason in my mind it was a federal court that had heard the case in Florida. Don't quote me on that. Perhaps the charges or evidence in this case weren't considered to meet federal guidelines and our district decided to do something about it anyway. One more thing to think about.

We heard the questioning of the defendant by his attorney, and then he was questioned by the prosecutor, the whole thing took approximately two hours. The defendant answered every question in a straightforward manner and with a level tone of voice. By the time the questioning was finished it was 4:45. The judge said we would adjourn for the day. Summations would begin the first thing on Friday morning.

When all of this jury duty stuff began, I thought I'd be home and finished by Monday night. The next day would be my fifth day. I thought I'd done my civic duty for a few years to come. I was ready to get back to work, and my wonderful friend Darla had to use five of her vacation days to fill in for me. How in the world would I repay her since she was adamant that she wouldn't accept payment for helping me, as she was getting paid vacation days from Rodney at Le Fluer? I had to think of something especially nice for her. Finally, I thought, "Oh, I know just what to do." Darla had shown she loved certain pieces of the pottery that was sold in my shop. I would purchase them myself and give them to her. Surely she would accept the pottery as a token of my appreciation.

As I was leaving the jury room there were four police officers lined up in the jury room hallway by the door to the regular courthouse hall. As we walked past, they asked us our names and looked at a list in their hands. I heard them ask several of the jurors to sit in a certain area so that they could talk with them. Clearly I wasn't on the list, since they let me go home. I would be giving my statement to Bolen that evening. Knowing him, he would ask a myriad of questions when he came by to take my statement.

On the way home I called the shop and they put me on speaker. I shared the news with Adelyn and Darla that I would be out one more day. I apologized to Darla, but she told me not to worry. "Girl, I'm happier than a fat tick on a hippo just doing my own thing without someone peeking over my shoulder to see every little thing I do."

"Well, I am more thankful for you than you can know," I told her.

"Adelyn and I are having more fun than two possums with a peck of sweet potatoes. You know that saying, 'When the boss is away,' don't you?" asked Darla.

"Are you trying to scare me?" I asked.

"Nah! Just funnin' with you. Any more news about John George?" Darla asked.

"I don't believe the police have discovered much about the case," I answered.

"I'm sure they're having trouble," Darla imparted. "They're like misguided rubber-nosed woodpeckers in a rock quarry right now."

Adelyn and I laughed, and we all said our goodbyes.

Bolen called me about 6:00 that evening. He asked if he could come by. I responded by asking him, "Have you eaten yet? I have enough roast with potatoes and carrots in my slow cooker to feed a family of ten."

Bolen answered, "I have not eaten, and I can probably eat enough for a family of eight. You have yourself a dinner partner. It's been a long day. What a good thing it is that your dinner partners only have to be a little more entertaining than your dogs." (I had forgotten about saying something like that.) "Can I stop on the way to pick up anything to go with dinner?"

I returned, "I'm pretty sure I have everything needed. Thanks anyway."

The dogs went crazy when Bolen arrived. He had learned

the hard way to stop and spend a little time giving each dog some attention, after which they were relatively content. If they didn't get that first bit of attention when a person entered, they could become super pests and jump around barking at whomever it was that ignored them. It took so little to please them, and yes, so little to frustrate them.

I gave Bolen my statement before I put dinner on the table. He seemed to think I had answered most of what he would want to know about the time on Tuesday before John George died. I was thankful. It meant I could enjoy dinner without having to think about and relive watching a fellow juror die from a seizure or from whatever had caused the seizure. I asked if the toxicology reports had returned.

"Not yet," Bolen responded. "They should begin coming in quite soon."

"Hey, have you ever seen the movie, *The Unsinkable Molly Brown*?" I asked. "I plan to watch it tonight. It's good sometimes to watch something campy to renew the mind when it has been overloaded with life-and-death situations."

"Is that psychology 101, Confucius, or Harri's helpful hints?" Bolen asked.

"It was more likely Harri's confusion," I answered. "Do you want to watch it with me? You know it's an oldie. Nineteen sixty-four."

"I must admit that I have not seen it," Bolen answered. "Sure," he said. "Why not? Let's watch it."

"Okay. Let's. It's about two hours long, so you can get home at a reasonable time," I noted.

Bolen was a good sport. I hadn't shared that it was a bit of a musical movie (okay, more than a bit), and I know musicals are not everyone's cup of tea; however, Bolen seemed to enjoy himself.

I arrived at the jury room early on Friday. I must admit that I was curious to hear what my fellow jurors would be saying about their talks with the police, and I wasn't disillusioned. Everyone was asking, "Did you talk to the police?" Thankfully when I was asked I was able to say yes. I did not want to appear to have been neglected by the police or to look as though I had received preference. Mr. Stare Guy across the table from me was not joining in the chatter, I noticed, although I could tell that he was listening. I used my outdoor voice to speak across the table and asked him, "Did the police speak to you too?"

He turned his head ever so slightly to look at me. He narrowed his eyes, grimaced, and said, "No discussion here."

I think he meant he wasn't discussing it with me. He could have meant that he hadn't spoken with the police; however, more than likely, he was talking about me. He obviously wanted to hear everyone else discuss it, though. It was almost like he was being a Peeping Tom, I thought. Before I had time to think any more about Mr. Stare Guy, we were called to line up for the courtroom; however, on the way, I walked by the chair where Mr. Stare Guy sat and saw the name that was written on his binder. Robert Goodson.

After we were seated, the summations began. The prosecutor had talked so much throughout the trial that, sad to say, I was a little tired of hearing his voice droning on and on. I had to work diligently to make myself listen carefully to what he was telling us. He told us to remember certain statements from a witness, but I knew the witness had not made those statements. He saw me shaking my head at him and mouthing "no." I couldn't tell if it bothered him or not. I have a very good memory, and had even taken notes on the particular circumstances he was speaking about. What he was saying was just not true. I realized that statements like those could sway a jury if the jury believed what the attorney was saying was true. A person could be convicted by attorney words and not evidence. Okay, that was scary. I wanted a truth buzzer to push when I knew something being said wasn't true. The jury should have had them. Truth buzzers. I wondered if I should put that suggestion in the suggestion box. I had to laugh at myself on that one.

Next it was time for the defense attorney. He said many fewer words and spoke slower. He wasn't wearing me out like the prosecutor. He mostly pointed out where he felt the prosecutor had not made his case. The prosecutor then got up again to give a rebuttal summation (I didn't know what the courtroom definition was for that; it was simply my take on the matter). It seemed he spoke the second time almost as long as he had spoken the first time. Did the judge give him grace to speak so long? I didn't know the courtroom rules.

The attorneys were finished. Finally. Thank goodness. The judge's charge to us as a jury was pointed and concise. We were then dismissed to begin deliberations. The huge responsibility had finally devolved onto us, the jury. It would be the first time we had discussed anything about the case among us. Everyone had been great about that point. The Law Clerk walked us back to the jury room. The Bailiff was ill and not in court that day. The Law Clerk was filling in for him. She told us that we were to pick a foreman, showed us a button to push and told us that it was a buzzer to the Bailiff's desk. We were to push the buzzer if we needed her, if we had any questions, or when we finished.

We knew so little about each other that no one knew who to pick for foreman. Everyone kind of muttered for a while. Finally after several minutes had passed one person said, "I'll do it." Whew! I could tell everyone was thankful that someone volunteered.

Everything was quiet for a time, so I announced, "I have something to say." All twenty-two eyes swiveled my way. I said, "I do not believe that the prosecutor proved his case. I don't know for sure whether or not the man is guilty, but we are supposed to decide on the proof of the case, and I don't think there was evidence to prove it."

Our newly self-elected foreman said, "Well, maybe we should take a vote. Who thinks the case was not proven and votes for a not guilty verdict?"

I looked around expecting it to be the start of hours of deliberation. Instead I saw every single person slowly raise a hand.

"Okay," said the foreman. Someone else said, "Write it down on the paper they gave us for the verdict."

Another person said, "Push the button so the bailiff will come back in. We need to let her know we have a verdict."

With all of that done, we had nothing to do but wait to be called back into the courtroom. I couldn't help wondering if we had broken some kind of a jury record in the speediness of our deliberations. The judge probably barely had time to leave the courtroom.

Everyone was speaking then. One person said, "I completely believed him, that he wasn't guilty."

Another said, "I thought the probability was that he was guilty, but there was no evidence to prove him guilty."

Everyone agreed again that the evidence was not there to support a guilty conviction.

We were called back into the courtroom, and the foreman delivered the written verdict. The judge read the verdict to the courtroom.

Can you believe it? I just sat there watching the judge read the verdict. My eyes did not wander off the judge. I have no idea how the defendant reacted to the verdict or how anyone else in the courtroom reacted. I missed my chance.

It was one o'clock. I headed the car toward my florist shop. Since I hadn't brought my lunch that day, I decided to use the drive-through at a fast food place. I took the food to the shop to eat, while spending some time talking with the girls.

When I arrived at the shop, the first thing I did was quietly put together a large box of pottery snuggled into tissue paper. I wrapped the box with some pretty ribbon and a bow and took the box to the back with me to give to Darla.

"Take this box home with you and open it there," I said to Darla. "Be careful with it, because the contents are breakable. And, thank you for being such a great friend and helping me out."

Julie, Adelyn, and Darla were all interested in hearing about the trial. They were also interested in hearing what I had to say about poor old John George.

It turned out that Darla had known John in college. She said he had a girlfriend that he later married, but girlfriend or not, he always seemed to be chasing other girls. That information was very similar to what I had heard from Amy.

I asked her about him gossiping. She shared that she tried to stay away from him but did remember hearing there had been some trouble. He had either threatened to tell or sell information he knew about someone. After talking for a while, I told Darla to head home so that she could relax a little before Lucas came home. I was more than looking forward to getting my fingers stained green with a little florist work. Working in my shop was relaxing to me after the week I had been through. Adelyn and I finished with all of the orders that needed to go out first thing the next morning and called it quits for the day.

One mystery of the week was more or less solved with our jury's not-guilty verdict. One more mystery to go. What did we know about what had happened to John George? Was he murdered? If so, who had murdered him or who had him killed, and why? What would show up first? We needed to know for sure that he was murdered, and then how. Next we would likely find clues as to why he was murdered, which would lead to who killed him. Who did we have as suspects? His wife and his family members would always be the first suspects to be followed up on or to be determined cleared. He seemed to be known as a womanizer. Had some husband taken offense to John's attentions to his wife? Or was it an unknown person that he saw on the way to the courthouse? How did one find unknown persons? Was it the defendant from our trial? Was it Mr. Stare Guy, or the person sitting directly to his right, Mr. No Name, or Sandra?

Did you notice how I used the word *we* four times? It was as if I was working with the police in carrying out the investigation. I was sure the police would quickly disabuse me of that idea. Truly I was thankful that discovering the guilty party was not my responsibility, but seeing someone die did give one a feeling of obligation to that person, didn't it? John George may, in fact, have been guilty of many differing misdeeds in his relatively short life, but it appeared that someone had played judge and jury and determined that John should die, and then that same person played executioner.

I determined that I needed to think back through Monday and Tuesday again to discern if I had left anything out of my statement that could make a difference. Did I see anything on Monday? I had previously written about only

Tuesday and Tuesday was the only day I had informed Bolen about when I gave my statement. I decided to go through each time period the jury was together in the jury room very thoroughly.

I shut my eyes and let my mind wander back to the beginning of the week. The first time I came into the jury room, Monday afternoon, I did see John already talking with several people. Yes, he even had his Yeti cup with him that first day. He spoke to Sandra on his left and to the man on his right, Mr. No Name, and to Mr. Stare Guy, the second guy to his right. He walked around some and talked to a couple of people at the end of the table to his right. When he walked back to his seat, Mr. Stare Guy said something to him. I remembered that John sneered and said, "You wish." We were then called into the courtroom and were there until time for us to leave for the day. No one stayed around talking.

I recalled that I went back to the jury room to leave my notepad with my binder on the table in front of my chair. The woman next to me was leaving her empty water bottle.

She said she would leave it so that she could refill it with water the next day. My eyes had swept the table to see if others were doing the same. I wondered if I wanted to do it also, as the three water bottles I had brought in my purse had been a bit heavy to carry around. I remembered seeing John's Yeti cup still on the table. That memory could be important, because it most likely meant that he had not brought coffee from home or stopped for some along the way. If he had coffee Tuesday morning in the jury room, he had most likely acquired it at the courthouse. If he came early, he could have bought something to drink at the café in the basement. Otherwise if he had coffee or water in his Yeti, it most likely came from our jury room.

I remembered talking with the three people on my right, Tuesday morning. Did I see anything or anyone having to do with coffee? I would have if I had looked straight ahead, because the coffeepot was in my line of vision directly across the table and behind the chairs of John George and Mr. No Name. I thought some more. I remembered a lot of milling around by the other jurors. The woman beside me was frustrated because her water bottle had evidently been tossed by the cleaning people the night before. I had brought another three bottles of water with me, so I gave her one of mine. Yes, her complaint had made me look to see if the Yeti cup was still there or if it had been removed. I saw someone holding the coffeepot and pouring coffee into John's Yeti cup. It was one of the people from the right end of the table. It didn't prove anything sinister, though, because he also poured coffee for Sandra. I'm guessing that the coffee was not the culprit. It was poison either administered to him at his home, given to him on the way to the courthouse, put into his Yeti cup at some point and mixed with the coffee, or a poison that in some way got onto his skin and was absorbed through the skin.

I realized that there was more that I remembered than I had given in my statement to Bolen. I decided to send a text to Bolen telling him that I needed to update my statement. I sent the text and then went to my computer to make the notes so I wouldn't forget them. Taking the time to reflect and seriously go back in my mind through those times in the jury room had definitely made a difference in my earlier remembrances. Did I have anything different to add to dates or times I had originally written about? The only thing standing out to me was the man who sat directly to John's right giving John a high five as he came out of the restroom, which seemed to be a strange thing to do. Of course I wasn't the high-fiving sort of person, so maybe it was strange only to me.

I remembered in the courtroom before the seizure began, John jerked like something had hurt him and he shook his right hand a few times. He then brought his hand up closer to his eyes as though looking at something. It was maybe only thirty seconds later when the seizure began. Could he have felt the beginning of the seizure in his hand, or could a needle have been placed under the arm of his chair with a poisoned tip? Okay, that sounded far-fetched even to me.

After I finished my revision I realized I was hungry and hadn't eaten. I knew I had some of the roast and potatoes remaining, and leftovers sounded good that night. After dinner I played the piano for a while. I was thankful that Mom and Dad had given me their piano. The boys didn't play, so Mom and Dad had exempted the piano from the sale when the boys bought the house. The piano was a baby grand that had belonged to my grandparents. I didn't play often enough anymore, but I always enjoyed myself when I took the opportunity.

Darla called to thank me effusively for her pottery. "I love, love, love it," she declared. "I opened the box and saw the beautiful pottery and said to Luke, 'Well, if that don't put cayenne in my gumbo.' Those were just the pieces I had been droolin' over."

Bolen called to say he couldn't come to take my revised statement, because he was working late. He said, "I'll try to get by sometime tomorrow. Is that okay with you?"

"Sure," I answered. "Whenever you can."

Bolen asked how things were and if we were finished with the trial. I shared some of the trial information and my thoughts about it with him.

He laughed and laughed when I told him about my suggestion-box idea. He said, "I needed that laugh. Thank you."

Sometimes I like it that I amuse him, and sometimes I'm not so sure. Actually I liked the suggestion-box idea. "I supposed I would leave out the truth buzzer, though," I reflected. Maybe I would send a letter to the court clerks with my thoughts or ideas. Why not? The court asked for me to give it my time to perform my civic duty, and I complied, so why couldn't the court—

"Harri, Harri," Bolen was saying, "are you running down one of your reflective rabbit trails?"

"Oh, Bolen, sorry," I responded. "I've been so much better about that this past year, haven't I? I guess I have had so many different things to think about this week that my mind forgot to stay in the present. It responded like it was the first driver past the checkered flag, who just kept going to do the winner's lap."

"Harri, you are capricious and whimsical tonight," Bolen announced, "and I think a little whimsy, at times, is good for the soul."

"Your soul or my soul? I don't think I've ever been told that I'm good for someone's soul. I kind of like that idea,"

I confessed. "Why are you working late tonight? Is there something new happening?"

"Thankfully nothing new," Bolen answered. "However, we do have some new information to follow up on about John George. And before you ask, no, I cannot share it with you."

"You're no fun," I commented. "I give my information to you. I guess with police it is always a one-way relationship."

"It does appear that way, doesn't it?" Bolen queried.

"Okay," I instructed him, "go back to work. Have a good evening. I'll just sit around my house and wallow in self-pity," I said, laughing.

Bolen laughed and said, "I truly doubt that. I foresee that before you even hit Stop on this phone call your brain will be taking off in one direction or another or in twenty directions at the same time. 'Night, Harri."

How right he was. Bolen must have received some lab results on John George. The poison was a fast-acting commodity; that I was sure of. If it was given to John George early in the morning, wouldn't he have shown signs before the seizure? Had it been before arriving at the courthouse, or would it have been around 8:30 or around 10:30? I fully believed that those were the times we were dealing with. I thought it could be either a form of arsenic or a form of cyanide. Both could be fast acting and cause convulsions, but so could some other poisons. I really wanted to know what poison it was. I could then think about the different ways of administering it and who could have administered it.

If the poison was administered through the skin, that scenario would be tricky. Something could have been spilled on his arm or hand or the poison could have been placed on his three-ring binder or Yeti cup. It could have been placed on the arms of his chair in the jury room or on the arms of his chair in the courtroom. It could even have been when Mr. No Name, who sat next to him, gave him the high five. I could not think of any other place where everyone else in the jury could not have touched. If he was the one expected to die, then the poisoner would have been careful in planning to make sure the correct person received the poison. Therefore, I eliminated the chair arms and the three-ring binder, because those could have easily been touched by someone else. That narrowed the number of ways that the poison could have entered his system through his skin.

I thought the best way for the poison to have been orally dispensed would have been in something he ate or drank at his house that morning or on the way to the courthouse. Someone could have put something in his Yeti cup in the jury room. At that time I could not think of another way for a poison to have been orally administered to John.

Who knew John George besides Amy and Darla? I texted both Darla and Amy and asked if either of them knew Robert Goodson, Mr. Stare Guy, or a redheaded woman named Sandra. I still didn't have a name for Mr. No Name. Amy said she knew who Robert Goodson was but couldn't tell me how she knew him. Her reluctance let me know that he had been a client in the law firm where she had worked. Darla said she knew a redhead named Sandra. I surmised the odds of it being the same person were slim to none. I had been hoping for a little information about those people, but

I doubted I would be able to get it that easily. I did, however, text Darla back and asked, "By any chance is the redheaded Sandra you know from your college days?"

Darla answered, "Yes, that's the Sandra that I knew. She was in college with us all four years. She used to go after everyone else's boyfriends so she wasn't the most liked girl on campus, by the other girls."

"Darla, do you think Sandra knew John George?" I asked, texting.

"Ours wasn't a big school, and everyone lived on campus," Darla responded. "It would have been difficult not to at least be aware of almost everyone there. So I would say yes."

"Thanks for the information," I texted back. "Oh, by the way, do you remember your Sandra's last name?"

"Her last name was Jersey," Darla responded. "I'm sure she must have married at least once, and I would not know what her name is now if she changed it."

I determined to look for Sandra Jersey on Facebook. Many women used their maiden names as their middle names on Facebook. It was worth a try. I would also look up Robert Goodson.

I found Robert Goodson on LinkedIn. It showed him as an investor in real estate. He invested; he certainly didn't appear to have the personality for selling. I wondered where his money came from to invest. His family? Had he worked hard to achieve it? Was he a slum lord? Was the money from illegal gains?

Sandra was on Facebook. Her name read Sandra Jersey Bachman Goldman. It stated her current status was single, but in a relationship. It showed no work history. Her college showed her field of study as fine arts. I was inclined to think that Sandra knew John George fairly well at college, if their fine arts degrees were in the same arts. Also Darla had mentioned it was a small college.

I continued looking online at poisons. Thallium could be used as a poison, although it wasn't often considered a fast death. I searched and discovered that I could order it online from Italy; thus it could be purchased easily enough. At one point in our history, thallium had even been used in a preparation to remove hair. Women had used it and had disastrous results from using it more than one time. As I thought about it I decided I wouldn't use thallium if I were looking for a speedy death result. John's death appeared to me to be one that happened within hours or even minutes from the time of ingesting or touching the poison.

Many people thought radium had healing properties, after the Curies discovered it. It was used widely in many things, even in makeup and toothpaste. It was eventually discovered to have caused many horrendous illnesses and deaths. I thought I could eliminate that poison as well as eliminate carbon monoxide from my list of possibilities.

I could have been much further ahead with finding who killed John George if Bolen had shared the lab results with me. The news media, having deduced that poison was used, was also trying to figure out which poison. The reporters were calling the murderer The Courtroom Poisoner.

I wondered if John George was on Facebook. I looked him up. Yes, that was him, an in-your-face kind of guy. He was tall with a large build, but not heavy at all. Instead of married or single, he listed himself as *looking*. I was curious as to how his wife felt about that. Every few posts he had this written, "Tell me what you know; it may be worth some dough." Someone bent on revenge would love to have a person who wanted to listen to his or her story and get it out in public. John had more than 4,000 "friends." He had plenty of opportunity to gain information and disseminate it.

There was one more person I wanted to look up before heading off to bed. I had decided to look up John's wife, June Berghoff George. Oh, my heavens! What a shock! The woman had obviously been the prize patient of some plastic surgeon. The result was a life-sized, disproportioned fashion doll whose plastic surgery looked to me as if it had exaggerated every feature of her face and body. I couldn't help questioning if she had brought about all of those changes anticipating that her husband would finally notice her. I felt sad thinking about her trying so hard to please John. I could only hope that the woman was pleased with what she saw in her mirror. To me she looked like a fashion doll that needed to be returned to the factory. Poor June. She had been mistreated from her high school years until now by John George. Just from curiosity, I researched fashion doll and discovered that the first fashion doll was owned by Isabella d'Este, mother to King Francis 1 of France.

I found myself liking John George less and less the more I knew about him; however, it didn't mean that the Courtroom Poisoner shouldn't be found. We can't go around poisoning people just because they aren't especially nice people. I had three possibilities, not including the defendant at our trial. The defendant could have gotten someone to do the job for him, even someone working at the courthouse. Courthouse employees were in and out quite often. I'm not sure now, though, that the defendant had anything to lose by leaving John George on the jury. If John knew something detrimental about our defendant and shared that information with the jury, we, could not have let that information make a difference in our deliberations. We had to make that decision based only on witness testimony and evidence. I decided I would eliminate the defendant as a possible suspect. The police could know more than I did about him, but from my standpoint, I was eliminating him. Oh, but maybe John telling the jury something negative about the defendant could have been seen as prejudicial which would have left it open for a mistrial. Hmmm.

"Hey, girls," I yelled. "Time for your last visit outside before bed. Let's go. Come on, get up." I had stayed up so late that I was having trouble trying to rouse them for their last outing, and they were not liking it. Eventually they all made it out the door.

After we were all back to our beds, I decided to read for a while to try to get the poisoner out of my head. I had a book list that I was working through. My current read was *The Idiot* by Fyodor Dostoevsky. It was a book that made me want to talk with someone else who had read it to see what others thought about certain parts of it. If you decide to read it, I suggest getting a friend to read it at the same time. I found, though, that it was not always easy to find others wanting to read and discuss old Russian literature.

Eventually I fell into a deep sleep. I dreamed about a tea

party being held in the jury room around that large table. We had lovely paper-thin antique French Haviland china tea cups trimmed with gold leaf and filled with yellow tea from China. John George was grinning from ear to ear and going to each cup and placing a drop of poison in it. We all smiled at him, even though we knew it was poison, and then drank the poisoned tea. Gradually, one by one, we laid our heads on the table in what we believed would be eternal sleep. Before I laid my head down, though, I thought, "I may be leaving this earth now, but I know where I am going, according to 1st John 5:13."

As we were all lying there, John began laughing. As he laughed, he said, "One of you poisoned me, and I know who you are. Everyone else but you may raise their heads and live." All of us but one raised our heads. I tried so hard to see whose head was still down on the table, but there was a napkin placed over the head, and I could not even tell if it was a man or a woman. I was quite frustrated. John just kept laughing and started ringing a bell. That bell was a great nuisance.

I finally awoke to realize the bell ringing was my doorbell. Who in the world was at my door that early on a Saturday morning? I picked up my phone to see who was outside. It was Rose and Florence, my nosy neighbors one and two. I spoke into the phone and told them I would be right out. I grabbed the nice robe that my brothers bought for me two years earlier and put it on. What time was it? I checked my watch and saw that it was eight a.m. I let the dogs out the back door and then made my way to the front door.

"Rose and Florence," I began, "how nice to see you this morning."

"We know you go to work a little later on Saturdays unless you have a big event, and we hadn't seen you leave, so we thought we would bring breakfast over to you," said Rose. Their arms were full of aluminum foil-covered pans.

Florence added, "And let you tell us about your week on the jury. That must have been exciting. I haven't been on a jury in at least twenty years."

That was it, wasn't it? They wanted the nitty-gritty about

my trial. They did not yet know about John George and me. They were in for a treat.

I plugged in my Keurig and poured in spring water so we could all have coffee. They had brought luscious-looking French toast covered with cinnamon butter. If needed, I had some real maple syrup to add to it. I retrieved the syrup container from the refrigerator, poured some syrup into a small pitcher, and warmed it in the microwave. They also had brought a bowl of mixed fruit and even hard-boiled eggs. In addition, I got out a gallon of milk. I must drink my milk in the morning, especially with having sweet foods like French toast with syrup. Their food was a treat for me, so I deemed it was a fair trade. Food for me and my stories for them. They swallowed my stories with as much relish as I swallowed their food.

When we were talking about John George, they asked me if I'd seen the movie *Arsenic and Old Lace*. I assured them that I had. I told them, "That is a favorite of mine. The one with Cary Grant."

Rose said, "Florence and I talked about that movie, and

we decided on the poison that we would have used if we had been those old ladies in the movie, although the movie title probably wouldn't have been as catchy."

"Yes," continued Florence, "we would have mixed up a batch of nicotine poisoning and given it to them in coffee instead of arsenic in homemade wine. We could even have served our homemade chocolate pie with it."

"You two are a hoot, or is that two hoots?" I asked. "Anyway, everything goes down well with that chocolate pie. I'll have to keep an eye out to see if you two start boiling cigarettes for the nicotine."

Rose and Florence *tsk tsked* about boiling cigarettes.

"I never know what you two will be up to next. I'd better keep an eye out for Mr. Larson," I said, laughing. "He hasn't been running up and down the street again in only his robe, has he?"

"He did that only twice," said Rose.

"Yes," continued Florence. "After the second time we called his son. His son now has someone living in the house with Mr. Larson to watch out for him."

"I'm sure that is a good thing," I stated. "Who knows where he might have ended up while wearing that short robe that didn't quite meet in the middle? He might have been picked up for flashing or some such thing."

Rose and Florence laughed, thinking about that possibility.

"You two will have to come over sometime, and we'll watch *Arsenic and Old Lace* together," I offered. "I'm sure I'll enjoy it more seeing it with you and through your eyes."

Rose chimed in, "Let's do that."

Florence added, "Just give us a call."

Rose said, "We'd better go and let you get ready to go to work. Thanks for sharing your time with us old ladies."

"Thank you for bringing me breakfast and giving me a cheerful head start to the day," I responded.

With that they left. They had already straightened up and put back in place everything in my kitchen that had been used and anything else they saw that appeared out of place to them. I let the girls in and fed them and my grouchy cat and then was off to the shower.

When I arrived at my shop there was quite a bit of noise outside, because my contractor was building a wood and adobe portico in the back for me. It looked like the workers were nearly finished. How I was going to enjoy that portico! It appeared that I had missed most of the noise while I was on jury duty.

We each owned our buildings in the business subdivision, but the association as a whole owned the rest. We had something akin to a home owner association, with an elected board, except we were business owners. My portico plans had been approved by the architectural committee. I wanted a covered place to park my car in case of hail and had not been sure the association would go for it. I came up with the idea of making my portico resemble all of our southwestern style adobe buildings, except even more realistic. The board was really pleased with the plan. I could visualize more of those porticos going up in the area. In fact, it would improve the looks at the backs of the buildings.

Adelyn usually took Wednesdays off. Since she had

worked all week while I was gone, she was not working that day, which meant I had quite a bit of work to do on my own.

I heard Julie yell, "I see a tour bus."

I yelled back, "If it gets too busy, let me know."

Thankfully the people were wandering around the area in small groups and there were no large groups coming in all at once; thus, Julie was able to handle the front while I worked on orders in the back.

At 1:00 I received a call from Bolen. He informed me that he would be working all day. He asked me if I'd like to bring the girls out Sunday afternoon. He said the girls could run in the pasture and I could go riding with him.

"I'm up for that," I quickly answered.

"Great," he said. "I'll see you about two o'clock tomorrow. I don't even have time to talk today."

At four o'clock Julie was ready to leave. She stopped in the back to tell me, "You may need to advise that Arizona potter to get a few pottery assistants, because we need to order a truckload of her work. We can hardly keep up with the purchases."

"I sure was fortunate to have met her just when she was looking for an outlet for her pottery," I commented. "I loved it and was sure others would too. It has been a big hit with everyone, since her pieces are distinct from other potters' work as well as different within her own work. It is all unique."

"I've even had to buy a few pieces for myself," Julie admitted. "Bye, now. I'm off."

That evening I pulled out another Cary Grant movie favorite of mine, *His Girl Friday*, with Rosalind Russell. The girls and I curled up on the couches and had a nice relaxing evening watching the movie. Listening to the overlapping dialogue was entertaining.

The next morning, I hurried off to my Sunday school class. I looked forward to it each week.

After church I made myself pimiento cheese spread. I shredded cheddar and gouda cheeses, mixed in the pimiento and some garlic, and added a mixture of cream cheese and a thick white dressing. Voila! Ready to eat. I decided to eat it with crackers instead of as a sandwich. I allotted myself five Ritz crackers and five Triscuits. It was a good lunch.

I didn't take the girls on their usual walk since we were going out to Bolen's, where they could run in the pasture. They were always excited to ride in the car. Most of the time they got to go to places that were fun. They definitely preferred not to go to the veterinarian. When at the vet in the dreaded examining room, they always stood staring at the door, ever hopeful it would open and they could bound out of the loathsome room.

We made it to Bolen's house. Bolen waved us over toward the pasture gate. The girls ran at full speed. I was afraid they would all jump on Bolen at once, which could be catastrophic. They behaved and seemed content with stopping in front of him to get petted, and then they took off running. They headed first toward the horse barn. They thought the horses were their big dog friends. Bolen and I headed for the horses too. The two we were to ride had already been saddled, so all we had to do was hop on and take off.

I loved the feeling of sitting in the saddle with the wind blowing through my hair as I rode.

After riding for about ten minutes, we slowed down and began to talk. "Thanks for giving me your updated statement," Bolen commented.

"Absolutely," I responded. "How's the case coming along?"

Bolen answered, "It's still frustrating. There are just too many possible suspects."

"I'm sure there are," I said. "I have even thought of a few myself, and I don't know the half of it. I have eliminated the defendant from our trial. I decided that if John George knew something about our defendant, it should not affect the verdict, since we had to make our decision based only on the evidence presented and not on a juror's statement."

"You have eliminated him?" asked Bolen, laughing. "Well, there may be truth in what you say. We are leaning that way too, but we have not eliminated anyone as yet."

I continued, "Did you know that John George was always finding out things about others and threatening to tell or sell what he knew? In addition, he had always been a womanizer, going back as far as high school."

"Really?" Bolen asked. "I should have talked with you earlier. You sound like you can solve my case for me," he said, smiling.

"Okay," I stated, "you can laugh at me, but I know what I know. My four possible suspects are Sandra Jersey Bachman Goldman; Robert Goodson; Mr. No Name, whose name I obviously don't know, who sat directly beside John to his right; and John's wife, 'Poor' June. Sandra, who was sitting directly to the left of John in the jury room, went to college with John, and they majored in the same field, although in the jury room she acted like she had never known him. Poor June followed John around in both high school and college, and he always went after other women right in front of her. He most likely continued with that M.O., because on Facebook he doesn't say he's married. He does say he's *looking*. Mr. No Name appeared fairly friendly with John in the jury room, and he's the one who high-fived John. He may have somehow poisoned John with his hand touch. Robert Goodson spoke to John and received a put-down answer from him. He was very strange in the days following the death and was extremely interested in what everyone had to say, although he wouldn't enter into the talks himself."

"Hey," Bolen commented, "you may have some information that I don't have. How do you know those things about John and Sandra?"

"Darla and Amy," I answered. "Darla went to college with John, Poor June, and Sandra, and Amy went to high school with John and June."

Laughing, Bolen declared, "From now on I'll check with you and your friends first for information on suspects. You got me this time, for sure. And, why is John's wife *Poor June*?"

"From what I have learned, it appears Poor June was humiliated by John almost her whole life," I answered. "I just feel sorry for her. I have a question. How do you decide if poison has been absorbed through the skin or taken orally?" I asked.

"I'm afraid I don't know the answer to that particular question," responded Bolen. "I do know that if a person ingests a poison that has a metal base, it may be able to be seen under x-ray. Otherwise, there are tests like the Prussian blue and Reinsch. Also I know there are some fast tests for showing the presence of poison, but to confirm which poison, tests must be run through gas chromatography-mass spectrometry. As to knowing if a poison is absorbed or taken orally, I simply don't know the answer to that question. It isn't in the police officer's handbook," Bolen said with a smile.

"I've tried and tried to figure out the poison that killed John George," I stated. "I've searched and read about almost every poison I can find. If the National Security Agency or some other agency is checking online to see who is researching poisons, or a few months ago who was researching pipe bombs and Molotov cocktails, someone may be coming after me before long," I disclosed. "In fact I've even come up with a couple of ways John may have been poisoned from something as easily obtainable as apricots and their pits."

"That sounds like you're giving someone a lot of credit for strong motivation and lab knowledge. You could be right, though," Bolen suggested. "However, we usually find that a person who has decided to kill uses the easiest means available to him or her. We'd probably have a lot more trouble finding the murderer if your apricot idea were the case. There would be nothing to follow up on, except grocery receipts." He laughed and said, "I think you'd make a worthy adversary. I want to stay in your good graces."

"Having watched John die, I have trouble not thinking about his death or wanting to find the answer," I remarked. "I thought if I knew what had poisoned him that I might be able to figure out who had poisoned him. I deduced that the time frame would be important as some poisons take longer to work than others, but now I'm not so sure. There are just so many possible poisons. He could have ingested whichever one it was at any time. Unless it was cyanide. I would have expected cyanide to have worked speedily. I know the police don't need my help, but still I keep trying, if only for my own satisfaction."

"We police usually think we can handle these things all by ourselves," Bolen admitted. "However, the truth is that without input from the community, we often would not know the right path to follow. I'll listen to your suggestions anytime."

We finished riding. After much coaxing, I had been able to get the dogs into the car. That was no mean feat, because they loved running in the pasture. I knew they would be ready for an early night after the afternoon's couple of hours of running, which made it a perfect night to have Rose and Florence over to watch *Arsenic and Old Lace.* I called and invited them before I left Bolen's property. They were excited about coming. I popped popcorn and even had time to stir up a batch of fudge before they arrived.

Cary Grant's facial expressions and antics were farcical and loveable. Rose and Florence were fun to watch and listen to also. Their quips were quite amusing. The evening went by quickly, and I was truly amazed at how fast my pan of fudge disappeared. We all three turned out to be chocolate lovers, and you can't beat my grandmother's fudge recipe. It melts in the mouth. I can just see you all running for popcorn or chocolate about now. I had made this recipe since I was a child; however, my grandmother still made it better than anyone else.

Monday morning I was out in the front of my shop replacing some bouquets when I looked up at the sound of the door opening and nearly dropped the vase I was holding. It was Sandra Jersey Bachman Goldman. "Well, hello," I ventured.

Sandra said, "Fancy meeting you here."

"Definitely unexpected," I answered. "But I own this shop. I am Harri."

Sandra commented, "Small world, isn't it? I was wandering around the area doing some shopping and remembered that a friend of mine told me that her daughter's wedding was decorated by Creations by Harri. It was a beautiful wedding. I will be getting married in two months and I'm hopeful you will agree to work on my wedding as well," Sandra revealed. "It won't be quite as large as the Spearman wedding was since it is not my first wedding, but I do want it to be every bit as lavish."

I opened up the calendar on my iPhone and typed in the date Sandra gave me. I asked her if she wanted to set a time to make floral decisions or if she was working with an event planner. She asked if I remembered who had been the event planner for the Spearman wedding. I was able to share with her that I did; it was Abella Roth. I gave her Abella's phone number. Sandra said that she would give her a call and either she or Abella would be back in touch with me.

I said, "We certainly were on jury duty at a difficult time, weren't we? I understand that you knew John George, and it must have been quite a shock to you to see that happen right beside you."

Sandra looked nonplussed and then finally said, "I did know of him during college, but you know who a lot of people are during college, don't you? You aren't necessarily friends with them, though, are you? He wasn't my kind of person then, and I had not seen him since college until I walked into the jury room. It was a surprise, and definitely not a pleasant surprise, as you may have guessed."

"The lady doth protest too much, methinks," as said in *Hamlet* by William Shakespeare. Those words came immediately into my mind while Sandra was talking. A simple yes or no would have been ample.

"Did you know anyone else on the jury?" I asked. "Did you get the name of the men sitting to the right of John?"

"Yes, I knew who Robert Goodson was, and I thought he acted very strange the entire week. At one time he was a friend of my first husband, that is until he tried to cheat him in a real estate deal. You couldn't get anything over on Desmond Bachman, though, as Robert soon discovered, to his detriment. The person sitting directly to the right of John, I did not know. I heard John call him Herman. He mentioned working for the state in some position. I remember it had something to do with the unions in the area."

"It was not the best week, was it, Sandra?" I asked.

"No, it was not," Sandra responded. "Not for any of us, especially for John, even though he was depraved. He mentioned he was fighting a migraine Tuesday morning and he hoped some over-the-counter meds someone had given him would keep it at bay. Not to appear crass, but he didn't have to be concerned about that migraine for long."

"True," I responded. "Back to our original subject. I will come up with some awesome ideas so I'll be ready whenever Abella or whoever contacts me about the wedding. Do you have the venue?"

"Yes, the wedding and the dinner will be held at Willow Marble Chateau."

"That's a beautiful venue for a wedding," I declared. "I will look forward to being a part of making your wedding magnificent for you."

"Thanks, I do appreciate it. As I mentioned, this is not my first wedding, but it is a very important wedding to me," Sandra said in parting.

I quickly sent off a longish text to Bolen. I had been made aware that texts and emails pertaining to police cases had to become part of the police paper trail so I tried to (when I remembered) to simply stick to the subject at hand. "Ran into Sandra from the jury. She didn't like admitting that she knew John George, but she did admit she had known him in college. She knew Robert Goodson, and she also thought he acted strange during our week together. She said Robert had been a friend of her first husband but was caught trying to cheat him in a real estate deal. Also, Mr. No Name, who you probably already know, is Herman someone. According to Sandra, he works for the state and his job has to do with unions. That's it. Enjoy your day. Oh, BTW, I'm going to be doing Sandra's third wedding. Ha." (Okay, that time I hadn't remembered.)

I was convinced more now than ever that Sandra knew John a lot better than she wanted to let on. Darla had said in college Sandra went after other people's boyfriends. She probably had a fling with John. Maybe she found out the hard way what a sleaze he was and wanted to wipe out the memory of that time in her life. I could understand that. I met a few sleazy men in college too.

A thought had just slipped into my mind. What if John had tried to blackmail Sandra in some way? Maybe caused her to lose out on a relationship she really cared about? And where were her previous husbands? I realized that I could not eliminate Sandra from my list of suspects. Would I still be her florist for her wedding? Of course I would. Accepting her money for my hard work was not something I would reject. She was only a suspect. Innocent until proven guilty; that precept entered American law through a Supreme Court decision in 1895, *Coffin versus U.S.* I found it quite interesting, because in actuality a person could be guilty of a crime, but according to law we must see them as not guilty unless it is proven beyond a reasonable doubt. The attorneys in the trial I just attended mentioned that in a criminal trial one could not base a decision on the preponderance of the evidence; it had to be beyond a reasonable doubt.

How quickly people often jump to conclusions when hearing chatter about someone! Often people don't wait for the tale they heard to be proven beyond a reasonable doubt or beyond any kind of doubt, do they? I've provided a lot of speculation while relating my story to you, but I will reach the truth before I finish. I don't want you to think that I misled you about any of the people involved.

I decided to hunt for more information about Herman. During my lunch break, that is just what I did. First I performed a search for his job. After several misses I discovered Herman Glotz. His job title was training and representative for the U. S. Department of Labor. Where had I come by the idea it was a state job? Oh, yes, Sandra had thought so. Once I knew his whole name, I could further search for him. I would have to do it later, as I needed to get back to work. Trying to solve crimes could definitely be time consuming, especially so when I worked and didn't have the resources of the police department.

Julie told me before I started back to work that someone had called asking what type of material we lined our caskets with. The woman said she was allergic to rayon and wanted to be sure we didn't use that material, as she would not want to have a reaction if she had an open casket at her funeral. Julie nicely told her that we didn't deal with caskets. Thankfully Julie had taken that call. I was concerned that

I might have answered something like, "We use silk for the lining, but stuff it with hay and ask, do you have hay allergies?" Sometimes my tongue works before my brain.

We do get some funny phone calls. They seem to come in batches of three around the new moon each month. I can't help questioning what kind of allergic reaction the woman thought she could have lying there in that unconditionally final environment.

Instead of thinking flippantly about the woman's question, I should have felt sorry for the poor thing. She truly had been concerned about the allergy to make the call. I wondered if I should call her back to relieve her worries and explain that she couldn't have a reaction when in a not-alive condition. But surely whoever she talked to who sold caskets would have made her aware of that. I decided I should quit woolgathering or daydreaming and get back to work. So I did. Back to work it was.

It began to rain as I was on my way home from work, and that meant no walk for the dogs. Only one of them didn't mind the rain. The other two couldn't be coaxed outside if there was a hint of a dribble, which indicated that we would be playing fetch the ball in the house to get exercise. I couldn't use a nerf ball, or they would chew it up, so I had to be careful how and where I threw the ball. I kept the house pretty clear of extra furniture and breakables as a rule, anyway, with having three big dogs and a clumsy cat.

Friday arrived. I was excited. The girls and I were going that afternoon to Amy's new doggie day care to check it out. It was the day before her grand opening which was planned for Saturday. Perkie, Joyful, and Hopeful were going to be able to try everything the day care had to offer, from playing, swimming, dog treats, the doggie spa, and the doggie beauty salon. Canine Sunset Vista was sure to be a big hit. One of the television stations and a newspaper was going to be there to get some close-up pictures of my dogs as they went through each area, which would be great advertising for Amy. I needed to remember to buy some newspapers Saturday and set my DVR to record the news. I assumed that Cian would be there Friday and Saturday also.

I did have to work that morning. The day wasn't

overloaded, but my plan to leave early meant I needed to go in to the shop early. I arrived at 6:30. It was so quiet at that time of the morning that I turned on the television. I was surprised to see Bolen on the morning news. He was being asked questions about the Courtroom Poisoner. I doubted that Bolen liked that moniker being used.

One of the newspersons asked, "A source told us that the poison used was one that acted within minutes. Can you confirm that?"

Bolen answered, "I cannot."

The newsperson then asked, "Do you have a suspect?"

Bolen responded, "We have several leads."

The newsperson kind of smirked and rolled his eyes and then asked, "Well, Detective Bolen, what can you tell us?"

Bolen answered, "I can tell you that the police department is putting forth every effort into finding the person behind the death of John George. We are gathering new information every day and are hopeful that before too much more time passes, we will be able to arrest the perpetrator. Unless someone is seen committing a crime and/or leaves a lot of evidence at the crime scene, finding a criminal takes a lot of old-fashioned detective work. We are endeavoring to discover as much direct evidence as possible, which we prefer to circumstantial evidence, although circumstantial evidence has its place. I hope I have answered your question sufficiently. Thank you for having me on your show. Now I must get back to work."

"Detective Bolen," the newsperson asked with a raised voice, "Do you have any direct evidence at this time?"

"As to evidence, I can't share that information with you. We value any evidence we come across to be sure that the correct suspect is arrested. We won't arrest anyone until we know we have the evidence necessary to ensure that what we pass to the District Attorney will be everything needed to pursue the case. We do not believe the perp is a danger to the community at large. That said, since we don't know that for sure, we are diligently working day and night to find the person responsible for the death of John George."

"Thank you, Detective Bolen," the newsperson said. "We look forward to learning just who the Courtroom Poisoner is and why he or she decided to take John George's life. From what I've discovered, Mr. George was a person with many flaws, and few morals, but he does deserve justice, all the same."

I performed a quick search on my telephone for Desmond Bachman. An obituary came up. It appeared that he died after two years of marriage to Sandra. He was sixty-six years old. I looked for Moses Goldman. Another obituary came up. They were married four years. He was sixty-five when he died. I thought I'd be a little leery if I were her new husband-to-be. I wondered how old he was. Both of Sandra's husbands had been millionaires. The first husband had three adult children who probably received the majority of the inheritance. The second husband, however, had no children. Sandra had to be around thirty-four, if she went to college right after high school and was there at the same time as John. She had definitely been busy.

I put in a search for Sandra's engagement announcement. It gave the name of her fiancé as Jonathan Alonso Patterson. I searched for him. He was an attorney aged forty-two. Maybe this marriage was actually a love match on Sandra's part. As to what had caused the deaths of her husbands, I did not know. The obituaries did not give that information.

I needed to get busy working and making floral arrangements. I had to save the rest of the research until later.

As planned I left work early and hurried home to pick up my three dogs. They did not know where they were going, but they were definitely excited to be going somewhere. They were probably thinking horses and pastures. I knew they would enjoy our destination as well.

Amy met me at the door of the building for big dog intakes. It was quite an amazing building, with all that it contained. We let some of the workers take the dogs out into the seven acres to run. The dogs were loving it. I saw Perkie head for the pool first thing and jump in.

Amy showed me around inside. I saw the little indoor-outdoor apartments for overnight guests. They looked almost inviting enough for me to stay in. The spa offered both muscle massages and paw massages, nail painting, teeth brushing, heated towel wraps, and undercoat deshedding. The beauty salon offered a hydro-massage bath, gentle blow dry, nail trim, and hair trim or full haircut of one's style choice. She explained that the small dog building offered the same services as the big dog building. My dogs even got to see the new veterinarian for a complete physical workup. She pronounced them hale and hearty. They didn't even seem to mind the visit, since they were the first dogs there and they could not smell the usual dog fear in the air or on the floor.

It was a wonderful experience. I told Amy to be ready for the onslaught of dogs, because her place would be an instant hit in the community. I was sure it would be.

We came home five hours after arriving at Canine Sunset Vista. Perkie, Hopeful, and Joyful looked gorgeous and smelled much better than usual. They were now going to be newspaper and television stars. Thankfully they would not know, so I didn't have to worry about dealing with puffed-up attitudes. Skinny's attitude was all the attitude I could take.

Skinny didn't have a day care to visit. She didn't even get to go to the pasture to play. I wondered if she would like to go to work with me some day for something different and to get away from the three dogs for a change. If I kept her in the back, I wouldn't have to be concerned with her getting out the front door. I decided to try that the next day, since it would be one of my shorter work days.

I did some searching again about Sandra's previous husbands. All I could find was that they had each died from heart attacks, or what appeared to be heart attacks. I wouldn't put it past John George to threaten Sandra, fact or fiction, about telling her new fiancé that the deaths were suspicious, which would definitely be a motive for her to get rid of John.

Robert Goodson, Mr. Stare Guy, I knew from Sandra was willing to cheat even a friend; thus I deduced that he would most likely be up to no good in other areas. There was obviously something he wanted John to change or not do from John's answer, "You wish." He also appeared to have a motive.

Herman Glotz, what about him? I wondered if he could be taking union money under the table to keep secret some piece of information he knew about the union bosses. I knew that was a stretch, but I did a union search in our area, anyway. An article I located said that the union leadership had been accused of choosing its disputes based on actions that would bring the most money into the union treasury. This tendency was letting the union leaders get rich, similar to the CEOs they often smeared when they could. The article stated that the leadership was not really concerned about the worker's welfare or conditions, but how they could make money. I knew it was conjecturable about corruption and Glotz, but it seemed to be something that needed to be checked into further.

I hadn't discovered anything untoward about Poor June. It appeared she had been too busy with her surgeries to get into much trouble. Of course that fact wouldn't keep me from continuing to look. I was sure that life with John had been difficult for her. I wondered where the money came from for the surgeries. Her family? Or John's money made illicitly? From what I could tell, she did not and had not worked outside of the home.

I sent an email to Bolen. I said, "I know this is all hypothetical, but here it is," and then I told him about my thoughts on the four possible suspects. After sending the email, the girls and I went to bed.

I had another tea party dream. Again people, including me, were all seated around the jury room table. This time our teacups were hand painted china with pictures of laboratories on one side and various pills and capsules on the other side. All the people were holding and looking intently at their cups. John, laughing, said, "The teacup always tells the story. Is the truth in the tea leaves? Or is the truth on the cup?" He laughed eerily. "You'll never know, will you? Drink your tea and see who is left."

We all dutifully drank our tea. As before, we all laid our heads down on the table.

John said, "Arise!"

We all arose except for one. That person's head was still down, but instead of a person's head, it was the head of a clown. John began singing part of an old song, "Send in the Clowns." At that point we all became dressed as clowns and began acting in clown-like fashion. It was quite bizarre.

John said, "Look for the silk lining in the casket. No," he said, "that's not right. Look for your connect-the-dots book. You'll find the answer."

I am not prophetic. The only thing my dreams did were to continue trying to find connections while I slept with whatever it was that I had been thinking about during the day. Sometimes I actually got good ideas from my sleep time. At other times, just a jumbled mess. The only obvious element that I concluded from that dream was to connect the dots. I knew I would definitely keep searching to see where the dots led, if anywhere.

No French toast on that Saturday morning. My nosy neighbors must have decided that I had nothing of interest to share with them that morning. I did give Amy a quick call to thank her for the girls and me for the day before at Canine Sunset Vista and to wish her the best day ever. I let her know that I would be praying for her.

I put Skinny in her carrier, and we headed to work. I fixed a spot for her at my shop so she could sit and look out a window. I placed her there, and she seemed content. The day was busy for a Saturday.

Abella called to let me know that Sandra had contacted her about the wedding. They had met and conferred on the wedding and dinner plans. Abella said that she needed to set a time to meet with me. She said she and Brad would like to meet on Monday, if that would work for me. We set the time at 10:30 Monday morning. "I also have something to show you," she added mischievously.

Abella and I had become friends several months before when we first started working together. We also went through some tough times together, which is usually good for cementing a relationship. Abella told me before ending the call, "Be ready for some over-the-top suggestions. This lady wants to wow her audience."

I immediately began thinking what to do for the wedding. I was sure that floral-and-crystal-covered candelabras on the bride's table would be beautiful. Oversized aisle arrangements for the wedding would give that wow factor. Garden-inspired floral displays hanging from the rafters would work for both the wedding and the dinner. Edible, organic flowers on the cake layers would give some flair, as would covering all the columns in floral displays. I'd add a tall metal stem, like a candelabra, with flowers hanging from it and set one on each table. It was a start. Between that day and Monday I had time to come up with additional suggestions. It was major work. It was essential that I hired some people temporarily for the wedding. It was crucial to get the word out quickly to find the kind of help I needed.

Bolen called around noon. He said it looked like he could get off around 6:00. He asked, "Would you be up for takeout from the Rib Cage?"

"You do know the way to this girl's heart," I answered. The Rib Cage was one of my favorite restaurants. "In case you didn't realize it, that answer was a definite yes."

"Okay, then. I should be at your place between six thirty and six forty-five. I'll even bring the dessert," Bolen imparted.

The day appeared to be a hit with Skinny. I concluded I would have to bring her to work more often. I decided to ask my contractor if he could come up with something fun and yet safe for Skinny at my shop. We did have to be careful with the flowers, as cats can be allergic to some flowers and others can be poisonous to cats. I had that information listed on my website for people sending us orders online. Also when we received a call for flowers, we always asked if the person to receive the flowers had a cat. Yes, dogs could also find some plants poisonous, but our flowers were usually set on tables where most dogs could not reach. For planting in one's yard, one should read about which plants are poisonous to dogs. I had that information also on my website.

When Bolen arrived he had food not only for us, but also he had stopped by The Meat Shop and picked up bones for each of the dogs. He handed them out as each dog was sitting, waiting expectantly, with their tails whipping back and forth dust-mopping the floor. As each dog received her bone, she ran to a different section of the house to enjoy her prize without interference from another.

By the time Bolen was through giving out the animal largesse, I had the food on the table. I even provided Wet Wipes with the stack of napkins. My two favorites from the Rib Cage were the Memphis dry rub and the Carolina sweet, but with just the slightest coating of the sauce. Our dessert was peach cobbler. Our ribs that time came with sweet corn on the cob, baked beans, and a tomato-cucumber salad in a vinaigrette with feta cheese. Are you hungry yet? Boy, I am.

We sat down to eat. I offered a blessing on our food.

While eating, Bolen asked, "Have you always been a Christian?"

I answered, "No. That's impossible. I had to understand that I was an unbeliever before I believed.

"That wasn't the short yes or no answer I was expecting," Bolen commented. "What then?"

I continued, "I came to understand that Jesus chose to die and take on our sins, even though He had not sinned. He took my place. It was a beautiful gift of grace."

"I think I understand now," Bolen stated. "Thanks for sharing."

We ate for a while in silence. Of course I had to ask about the case. I wouldn't be me if I didn't. "So, any news on the John George case?"

"I read your hypothetical email. Actually, believe it or not, it did give us some ideas for follow-up," Bolen confessed. "Sometimes it's good for us to have someone around who thinks outside the box."

"Is that a nice way of saying that my way of thinking is skewed?" I asked.

"Maybe," Bolen responded, laughing, "but I followed an idea from you before that eventually brought us to a result. Those ideas of yours just may bring us a solution again. We will just have to wait and see."

"Thanks for sharing that. I feel better now," I remarked. "Any other news that you can share with me that you couldn't share on television?"

"You never quit, do you?" asked Bolen with his lopsided smile. "Let me think a minute. I can tell you that the heirs to Sandra's first husband requested a full autopsy. The physicians doing the autopsy found no suspicions of any kind. Also Desmond was known to his doctors to have cardiomyopathy. As far as Mr. Goldman is concerned, we have no such information. Concerning Robert Goodson, we found his name and phone number in John's phone. If John had some information about him that Goodson didn't want known, we haven't discovered it as yet. Herman Glotz, we are also moderately investigating. We're checking with someone in the unions who is a snitch for us. How'd I do?"

"That was very informative," I admitted. "I appreciate your sharing that with me. I really do; however, can you share anything with me about the poison?"

"You not only don't quit, you are never satisfied," Bolen expressed, laughing.

This time I was thankful that he was laughing and wasn't exasperated with my questions.

"Remember that old saying, 'I would if I could, but I can't?' That's it. I cannot tell you anything about what caused John George's death."

"Okay," I remarked. "I just had to try. You don't find out if you don't ask."

"Except in this case," Bolen specified. "You asked and still didn't find out." He smiled then.

"That's true. I'm like my Redbone Coonhound. When my nose gets hold of a scent I can't stop. I just keep going wherever the scent takes me," I explained. "Hey, do you have time to watch a movie? I have both the nineteen eighty-seven movie and the two thousand eighteen remake of *Overboard*. Have you seen either? The original is about one hour and forty-five minutes. The twenty eighteen version is one hour and fifty minutes. They're essentially the same, and yet different."

"Tell you what, let's watch the original movie tonight, and the next time I come over we can watch the twenty eighteen version. How's that?" Bolen asked.

"Sounds great," I answered. "After all of that food and the peach cobbler, I'm not up for popcorn. How about you?"

"I'm fine as I am," Bolen responded.

We had an enjoyable evening. Bolen put his arm around me, and I snuggled up comfortably against his arm. He laughed watching the movie, and his laughter made me laugh too, even though I had seen the movie before.

On Sunday afternoon I worked on the plan to present to Abella for Sandra's wedding. For purely selfish reasons I hoped Sandra wasn't guilty. I would work for her, presuming her to be innocent, but I hated to think that I could be working for a murderer. Ostensibly it meant I must have been pulling for one of the others to be the guilty party. My list of suspects might have had nothing to do with killing John George. It could have been any number of other people. I finally finished what I thought was a great plan for a lavish and yet unique wedding from a floral standpoint. After a lot of work for the wedding, I sadly spent a lot of time with my nomadic mind running down many a suspect's passageway chasing after that elusive murderer.

Amy called. "Harri, you'll never guess," she declared. "Cian and I are engaged."

"Wow!" I answered with enthusiasm. "I wouldn't have

guessed, but I am not surprised. I am so excited for you. Tell me all."

"I'll call you tomorrow," Amy said. "Cian is still here. I just wanted to tell you first. We are so happy."

"Wonderful, my friend," I said. "I will look forward to hearing every detail when you call tomorrow."

I went to bed, and while I was reading *The Idiot*, I was even hopeful that the book might help bring about a connection of some of those dratted disconnected dots for me. The major character was full of goodness (big difference here), but those around him were full of guile. John George wasn't naïve and gentle, but it appeared that those around him weren't either. I had the strangest feeling all of a sudden that there was someone else missing from my suspect list. I also speculated about the dots. Could connecting the dots mean connecting the suspects? Could they have found out about each other, that John was threatening them, and then decided to work in tandem? There was something else that I had heard or read that could make a difference, but it wasn't coming to the forefront of my brain at the moment.

It was like other niggling thoughts I had experienced during previous situations that involved the police. I hoped I would remember it soon.

On Monday morning, while eating my one egg, one piece of toast, and one piece of bacon breakfast, I searched the news on my phone. I was rather shocked with what I discovered. Robert Goodson had been found dead. Interesting. I thought, "Ay, now the plot thickens very much upon us." A line from the play *The Rehearsal* by George Villiers, 1671. What did this new development mean to the case?

I sent Bolen a text saying, "Have you considered that some of the suspects may have worked together to poison John George? I'm not excluding Robert Goodson, even though he is dead, and I am assuming that his death was perpetrated by nefarious means."

Bolen had been busy. In going through some of John George's papers he found something alluding to a storage rental space. After the police called many storage rental places in the city to discern if John had rented a space with them, they discovered that storage rental companies would not reveal whether or not a person rented with them unless they were served a warrant.

When asked by the police, John's wife told them that she was not aware of any rented space. She said that John was very secretive about some things, so it wouldn't surprise her if he had rented a place she didn't know about. The police simply were trying to locate the storage facility, which meant the warrants would need to be carefully worded to get a judge to sign off on them. Each facility would need to be listed, and the warrant had to indicate the name of John George. Another warrant would need to be obtained to enter the rental space, if and when the police discovered that John had indeed rented a space.

First things first. There were twelve storage rental businesses in our city. Six warrants were written and attested to for six businesses. The six additional storage places were not receiving warrants that morning. If the first warrants did not achieve the desired result, the police would try to obtain the next six warrants. The warrants had been taken to a judge's office where they were, thankfully, signed. Police officers were assigned to deliver the warrants to the businesses and were soon dispatched to do so.

It turned out that none of those businesses had a John George as a renter.

Bolen was concerned that John could have rented a space under a pseudonym, but he was not feeling defeated. There were still six businesses to go. Bolen wrote out six more warrants and had them attested to. Those warrants were also taken to a judge for signatures. This judge asked quite a few questions, but finally determined that the information could be pertinent to finding a murderer; thus she signed the six warrants.

As before, those warrants were dispatched to the businesses by police officers. The police involved with the warrants felt luck had been with them that day. They discovered that John George had rented a unit at Purple Lakes Storage Sense. Another warrant was written and attested to and would be sent over to a judge first thing Tuesday morning, so that the police would be able to search John George's storage unit.

Amy called as soon as I arrived at work. She was elated, and I was truly happy for her. She said she was going to text me a picture of her beautiful ring. She actually did share every detail with me, I'm sure, building up to the moment Cian asked her to marry him. Amy was such a delightful person. Of course I asked about the wedding. She answered that they were looking at next September. That was ten months away, which sounded to me like big wedding plans would soon be in progress.

I worked diligently until Abella and Brad arrived for their 10:30 appointment. We sat around a small table with workbooks and laptops piled up in front of us. We were throwing ideas back and forth at each other, when I noticed something big and bright on Abella's left hand.

I stopped right then and said, "Abella, what is that on your ring finger?"

Abella laughed and said, "That is what we had to show you. Brad and I are engaged."

"Wow, just wow!" I spit out. "Now that is exciting, and I am completely surprised."

"Several months ago, when Brad did something daring just to save me, I realized how much he cared. Then before long, I realized that I cared about him too. I'm so thankful that I understood it then and quit running around looking for love in all the wrong places, or at least from all the wrong people," Abella shared. "We are so excited. Our partnership will be part of our life now and not just in business."

"Brad and Abella," I stated, "I am so very happy for you both. Such wonderful news." I gave each of them a hug.

"Now back to the mundane," I said, "and Sandra's wedding. Actually, there is nothing mundane about Sandra's wedding, is there?"

Abella and Brad both laughed and agreed. It did not take us much longer to decide on my part of this lavish wedding. They both approved of my plan, completely.

When the police arrived at Purple Lakes Storage Sense on Tuesday, they found a five-by-five storage room had been rented. It contained a large old wooden desk with a cheap black LED lamp on top along with a well-used fake leather chair with a slit in the back and on rollers that were a little bent. There was also a file cabinet, painted, but scratched; however, it was obvious that someone had been there before the police, as papers were strewn around and the middle drawer to the file cabinet was left open. All of the file drawers had been pried open with something like a crowbar, so forensics was called to come out to check for evidence. After that they placed all of the papers in a box and took them back to the police department for further review.

The police were astounded at some of the materials they found in the files. John had collected information and had files on more than one hundred people. There were documents and pictures in some files. Many of the files did not have direct evidence, but simply had papers detailing what John knew about them. From John's desk they had discovered a book showing how much money he had received and from whom. Actually it didn't show exactly from whom, as there were only initials written down, but the police were hopeful to match the initials with the files they had confiscated. There were no files gathered from the storage space on Goodson or Glotz. Either there were none or they had been stolen during the break-in. In the money book, however, they did discover the initials of R. G. and H. G. with moneyed amounts beside the initials.

By late Wednesday the police had matched all the files with initials in the book except for the R. G., H. G., and there was also an H. R. that did not have a file. There was an S. J. in the book, which referred to Sandra Jersey, Bolen noticed, but that file had not been taken by the thief.

Bolen came by Wednesday evening. He said, "Harri, I've got to give you credit. With some of the evidence we have, or to be more exact, don't have, it is looking like there may be something to your idea about the suspects working together. There is no proof of it, as yet, just supposition and a kind of connecting the dots."

"Connecting the dots. That's exactly what made me arrive at that assumption," I answered. (That, a dream and a book by Dostoevsky, I said to myself. Some things are not meant for sharing.)

"I'm going to talk with my captain tomorrow about letting my team handle the Robert Goodson murder case, as well as the John George case. I believe we are going to find a link between the two cases that may not be proven if they are worked on by a separate team," Bolen divulged.

"I certainly hope that your captain can see how those dots connect," I commented. "Let me know."

"Oh, did I tell you that my friend Amy is engaged?" I asked Bolen. "You remember Amy, I know. You also met her fiancé, Cian, a few months ago at the singles event we attended. Not to be outdone, Abella and Brad are also engaged. I did not see that one coming. But I'm really happy for all of them. Oh, and did you see Perkie, Joyful, and Hopeful in the newspaper or on television? They are now celebrities."

"I must admit that I haven't seen any television recently, but I did catch sight of the girls in the newspaper," Bolen offered. "If I know you, you recorded their television debut and will show it to me later. Am I right?"

"I did record it and will be pleased to share it with you," I admitted.

"And I assume this is all good news about your friends, Amy and Abella?" Bolen asked.

"Yes, I do believe it is," I answered. "Abella and Brad became engaged on Friday night, and Amy and Cian became engaged on Sunday night. That was a big weekend for my friends. I am pleased for them."

I changed the subject. "Do you have anything more to share on the case? I can't let you off the phone without my usual inquiries, can I? You might think it was someone else you were speaking with if I didn't question you."

"And here we were having such a nice, pleasant conversation. We were talking like two friends, not like a policeman and a woman who finds dead bodies. Wasn't it nice?" Bolen asked.

"Okay," I uttered. "I give up."

"You think I'm going to believe that?" Bolen asked, laughing. "Not on your life."

"Then just go ahead and tell me everything, and I won't have to ask any more questions," I stated.

"You not asking questions? That is not a possibility. It can never happen," Bolen alleged.

"You may be right," I answered, laughing.

"I'll share one thing with you," Bolen said. "We found where John George kept some of his information, and we also found Robert Goodson's fingerprints at that scene. That's it. No more."

"Yes, yes, yes!" I expounded. "I knew they were connected in some way. Yay!"

"What fun you are," Bolen admitted. "I can't imagine many dull moments with you around."

"Is that scary?" I asked.

"No, not to me," Bolen responded. "I'm a police detective. We thrive on a lack of tediousness."

"Oops, my mom is calling to Facetime with me," I shared. "I'd better take the call."

"Go ahead," Bolen said. "I've got to run along anyway. I'll let myself out. Bye."

I talked with my mother and father for about half an hour. They are still in love with their retirement life in Mexico. Sometimes Mom forgets and speaks to me in Spanish. I studied Italian in college so I can understand some of her language lapses. My parents are completely settled into their new life. I am happy for them. Mother implied that they would be coming for a visit sometime in the next few months. I hadn't seen them in a little more than two years. I couldn't go to Mexico because of the court case for which I had been subpoenaed and after that, another situation came up at my home and shop, and then I was busy growing my new business. Maybe I'd get to visit with them in Mexico the next year. I knew it would be great to see where they lived and meet all their new friends. I needed to take a course in Spanish before heading to Mexico.

Thursday morning started out feeling like winter was getting close. There was a definite chill to the air, which was not surprising, since it would be Thanksgiving in two weeks. I wondered if I should invite some neighbors in for Thanksgiving dinner. I could invite my brothers too, and

Darla and Luke didn't have any family close by. I had a table that seated twelve, fourteen in a pinch that I had inherited from my grandparents when they downsized. If I was going to do this, I needed to get started with invitations. I called Darla and left a message. I called William and then Oliver and left messages. Did no one answer their phones in the morning? I called Florence and then Rose, neither of whom ever missed a telephone call. Rose was invited to a cousin's house for thanksgiving, but Florence was very pleased to be invited. I would wait for answers from those I left messages for before inviting anyone else. Oh no, I needed to invite Adelyn and her husband, Gabriel, as they didn't have any family in the area either. Their families were coming for Christmas. Well, I would wait to hear from these.

All four girls were fed and then had their last outside time before I had to leave for work. Skinny always wanted out with them, but I couldn't take that chance. She was not a street-wise cat. Thinking of being street-wise made me think of drugs, which made me think of what had been niggling at my brain. It was Sandra mentioning John's migraine and that he told her he had obtained some medicine that he hoped would keep it at bay. Could that medicine have anything to do with his death? But who would have known he was going to have a migraine and come prepared to give him medication? Nope, that didn't make sense at all. As with the previous time I had this brain niggling, I wasn't particularly eager to tell Bolen, because it didn't appear to have any credibility to it; however, I was feeling as though I should tell him about the medicine, just in case he had not previously been made aware of it.

Thus, my text to Bolen said, "I doubt if this means anything, but I just remembered something that I've been trying to remember for several days that Sandra Goldman mentioned to me. Can you meet me at my shop this morning?

Bolen and I arrived at my shop at exactly the same time. After greeting each other, I shared that Sandra had told me the morning John George died he had disclosed to her that he was fighting a migraine. He told her he had gotten some over-the-counter medication from someone, and he hoped it would help to keep the headache at bay.

"That's it," I stated. I'm not sure how that information is helpful, since I can't understand how someone could have known that John would have a migraine; however, maybe you can check with the people who worked for that jury room off the hallway as well as the other jurors to see if anyone saw him get meds from anyone."

Bolen said, "Thanks. That is new information. By-the-way, I received approval for my team to work on the Robert Goodson case also."

I said, "That's great. Here's a reward to your persistence," and handed him a couple doughnuts.

I had run a little late that morning leaving no time for breakfast. Thus I had run through the Krispy Kreme drive-through and picked up two dozen doughnuts. When warm they simply melted in one's mouth. I had decided that Adelyn and Julie might appreciate them as well as the men working to finish my portico. It was possibly even their last day of work, I thought. The portico looked gorgeous.

I had been right. Everyone loved the Krispy Kreme

doughnuts. I remembered that they had been a favorite of Rodney's at Le Fluer. My portico was finished except for a few finishing touches of paint. I could begin parking there the next day. I was definitely pleased.

I had been so busy with phone calls and texting that morning that I hadn't checked the news. I turned on the television at work to a local news station, just in case something interesting came up during the morning. At 11:30 the news showed the police going into Robert Goodson's home, and at the same time the police were going into his office. I probably wouldn't get to know if they found anything of interest. I wondered if they had associate police people. I'd sure want to be one, if I could get information given to me. I'd be like a helper or an assistant. I doubted they hired florists to consult with. Too bad. It would have been a win-win. I would give them my expert opinions, and they in turn would give me vital information. I knew it could never happen, but it was fun to dream about.

I wondered if Bolen had to work late. I desired a little more enlightenment about the case. I thought if I took a really nice dinner to him then maybe he would feel compelled to share information with me. Yes, okay, I saw myself for what I was. I was obviously ready to become a schemer, and it wasn't a pretty sight. Just for that I should take dinner to him and not ask any questions and tell him not to share anything with me about the case ever again for my punishment.

My phone rang. It was Bolen calling to say that he would be working late that night, but he was going to take a couple hours off for dinner. He asked if I wanted to have dinner with him.

"Yes," I answered. "I would like dinner with you, but you can't tell me anything about the case. I have a confession. I was almost ready to put into action a scheme simply to get some answers from you, but then I realized what a terrible person I must be, so I had to tell you not to tell me anything... as a punishment."

Bolen laughed so hard I thought he might choke. "I have been on the police force for several years now, and it is difficult for anything or anyone to surprise me. Harri, you can do that. You can surprise me. Almost anyone else would have wanted to keep that bit of news to themselves, but you come right out with it. I love it! Okay, since I'm on a tight schedule, do you mind meeting me at the restaurant?"

"I'm fine with that," I commented. "Did you have a place in mind? If not, how about that little East German restaurant? I think you liked it."

"That sounds good to me," Bolen answered. "Does six o'clock work for you?"

"Sure," I responded. "I'll meet you there at six."

I worked extra hard the rest of the day so that I could take off by 4:45 to get home, feed the dogs and let them out so that I could enjoy my dinner with Bolen without being concerned about them. I took the dogs out into the yard and threw sticks for them to retrieve. They loved chasing sticks. They didn't often bring them back to me to throw again. Sometimes I got more exercise out of those tossing games than the dogs did. Thankfully being home also gave me a little bit of time to touch up my hair and makeup. Yes, I definitely needed it.

When I arrived at the restaurant, Bolen was waiting outside for me. He hugged me and said, "It's such a treat to see you. It has been a busy week."

I was sure I had never been a treat for anyone before, especially after I had just confessed my incorrigible personality to them. I hugged him back, although I didn't know what to say.

We were able to get a table right away, and it didn't take us long to order our food. After ordering, I gave my menu to the wait person and smiled across the table.

Bolen asked, "Have you ever heard of Hadrian Rose?"

"The name doesn't ring a bell," I answered. "If I think of something later, I'll let you know."

"No questions?" Bolen asked. "You were serious, weren't you?"

"Yes, I was. I am," I responded. "I didn't like the person I saw...that me, primed to be devious."

"Okay, tell me about your parents. How are they doing? I know you spoke with them last night," Bolen said.

"Mom said to tell you, hi," I stated. "They are happy

and having a great time with all they are doing. Mom even forgets and speaks to me in Spanish every once in a while. I miss them. Hey, I'm having some people over for Thanksgiving dinner. I thought you might have plans to be with your family, but I wanted to let you know that you are invited."

"As a matter of fact my parents and my sister and her family who live here in the city are going to my other sister's home in Ohio for Thanksgiving. I don't get any day off except for the Thursday of Thanksgiving, so I can't go with them. I appreciate being invited and I accept," Bolen disclosed.

"Great!" I declared. "I heard from Darla that they will be coming. Also, Adelyn and Gabriel will be there. Oh, and Florence. I'm waiting to hear from the brothers before I invite anyone else. I'll get a huge turkey, and I like making dressing. I imagine Florence will bring a couple of her and Rose's famous chocolate pies. It makes me hungry for them just thinking about them. Too bad homemade chocolate pie isn't a famous East German dessert. Here I am stuffing myself with this scrumptious sauerkraut potato salad with the wonderful homemade vinaigrette, and I'm practically drooling over chocolate pie."

"I happen to know a place not too far from here that makes great homemade pies," Bolen disclosed. "Let's run by for dessert. I have enough time. Do you?"

"Yes!" I answered. "I already took care of my family. Why didn't I know about this pie place?"

"Because we police like to keep it our own little secret," Bolen responded.

I laughed at that. "Separate cars or one on this little foray?" I asked.

"It's close," Bolen answered. "I can drive and then drop you back at your car. How's that?"

"Let's boogie on out of here," I said. "I know, nineteen seventies slang."

"When did you decide you liked all things retro?" Bolen asked when we got into his car.

"The short version?" I asked. "When I was around five years old. I saw a retro dress in a thrift shop that I fell in love with. From that point on, I found that I was drawn to things that showed character. For me, that was retro or things created in the past."

"You know," I continued. "For some reason, even though I was rather shy when I was growing up, I never was concerned about what other people thought about what I wore. In fact I started all kinds of fads in high school. I would wear something I liked, and before long other girls were wearing the same or similar thing."

"Here we are," commented Bolen, "Pie in the Sky."

While we were eating some tremendous slices of pie (yes, I had chocolate), we chatted amicably about some things that were in the news regarding our city. Our city had been researching the publicly owned fast-speed internet in Chattanooga, Tennessee. It was fiber optic and appeared to have been great for the city and the people there. It surely sounded good to me. Our city fathers and mothers believed that they could surpass the speed of Chattanooga's internet. The other big news was a new lane on the interstate between our city and the state capital. The interstate could become a logjam, because many people drove from our city to the state capital or beyond each day for work, and in the summer, our interstate was also filled with out-of-state travelers.

As Bolen was driving me back to my car, he said, "I appreciate that you are punishing yourself; however, for your good behavior, I am going to tell you that your conspiracy theory is holding water. We have, in fact, found evidence of a connection of the dots. That's all that I will say."

"Thank you for that," I answered.

Once I was in my car and headed home, I realized that I was pleased that I had let Bolen know my thoughts about connecting the dots. It was looking like there was some basis to it. At times I had questioned whether or not to tell Bolen what I was thinking about a case. I remembered: "Our greatest weakness lies in giving up. The most certain way to succeed is always to try just one more time," a quote by Thomas A. Edison. Perseverance and facing our fears were almost always good character traits.

On Friday morning, I took Skinny to work again. My contractor had made a small indoor-outdoor area at the back of my shop for Skinny to run around in and enjoy. It was an area that was screened-in so she would think she had freedom. I hoped it worked for her. I was almost certain that she would love the outdoor area. With the new arrangement I didn't have to be concerned about her getting into any flowers that could be harmful to her.

At five to eight, the news came on the car radio. The newscaster was talking about Robert Goodson. It was deemed that his death had come about from being attacked by a poker from the fireplace in his office. The curved part of the poker appeared to have caused the initial damage. Ouch! He obviously had not seen it coming. Since it was his own poker that hit him, it seemed it was not a murder that had been planned ahead of time. Robert had made someone angry, was my guess. He had most likely pushed that person a little too far. I wondered if we could all reach that point, that point where we just couldn't take any more, and before we knew it, we had harmed someone or even killed someone, as in this case. I knew we didn't like to think those things about ourselves, but I supposed it was possible. Chilling.

Skinny appeared to like her new play area. I knew getting away from the three dogs once in a while would be pleasing to her, although they rarely bothered her. It was as if they knew that she was the alpha dog, or top cat, as the case may be.

I continued to think about Robert Goodson while I worked. I had thought that he was in some way connected to John George's murder. I wasn't ruling it out, either, simply because he had been killed. What was the name Bolen had asked me about the previous night? It was somebody Rose. I remembered that it had something to do with a fence or a wall. That was it, Hadrian's Wall, which was in England. His name was Hadrian Rose. I didn't know why he asked me about him. Was he in some way connected?

I did a search on my phone for Hadrian Rose. I found another obituary. He had died two years earlier at the age of forty-nine. That was young. The obituary did not indicate how he had died. Wait! At the bottom it said "In lieu of flowers, please make donations to the International Suicide Resistance Association." Hmmm, I thought. He must have committed suicide. Why would someone who committed suicide have anything to do with either case? Of course Bolen did not say Hadrian's name had anything to do with his current cases; however, those were the cases he was working on. I'd see what else I could find out about him that night, I decided. There was something about the obituary that was causing that old niggling in my brain again. I knew better than to try to get at it right then. It would come to me later when my mind was relaxed.

I was fortunate in finding some temporary help for the week of Sandra's wedding. Two women who had previously worked in florist shops but were now staying at home with their children were looking to make a little extra money. I thought it would be relatively easy to teach them what I wanted them to do. I would even get Julie working as much as she could with flowers during that week. It would be good if I could find one more person to help with the actual decorating. Perhaps someone else would answer my ad.

After arriving home I discovered my answering machine, Mr. Voice, was blinking. I almost forgot to look at Mr. Voice, because most people had my cell number and used that number to call me. Mr. Voice was an anachronism that I enjoyed. He used to belong to my grandparents. First I had to feed the dogs and let them outside, and then I could attend to Mr. Voice. That night not only were the dogs eager to eat, but they also had to smell Skinny after I took her out of her carrying case and placed her on the floor. The dogs had never been to my shop, so they had no idea what they were smelling and couldn't tell where she had been, but not for lack of trying. Finally Skinny growled at them, and they all backed off. They knew that when she growled she meant business.

I picked up a pad of paper and a pen and pushed the button on Mr. Voice. Lo and behold! It was Gilbert Tarleton. Gilbert had lost his home and his florist business from acts of arson. After last speaking to his wife I had assumed they had moved away from our city. Gilbert's message said he had purchased an entirely different type of business after the fire had taken his florist shop. He said the good and the bad of the new business was that it could almost run without him. He indicated that he would be delighted to help out the week before the wedding. His wife had shared with him that my hospital visits and telephone calls had meant a lot to her while he had been incapacitated, so he was especially looking forward to being of service. He also stated that he missed staying busy.

I picked up the phone and called him right back. We had a nice chat. It was good to talk with him and to hear that he and his family were doing well. We made arrangements for him to work the week before the wedding.

Life was so interesting. People thread in and out of our lives at different times. I found it to be like a tapestry; people weaving in and out, bringing with them the various colors and textures of their lives that made our life tapestries beautiful. I loved that thought.

Meanwhile, Friday was busy for Bolen. The poker that had killed Robert Goodson had been wiped, but there was one small fingerprint in blood that the murderer had not removed. It had probably been overlooked in the murderer's haste to leave the premises. Obviously that print had been sent to forensics and the information had already returned. The print had been run through AFIS, but to no avail. It was the print of an unknown person.

The police had been busy going through papers and items from both John George and Robert Goodson. It was extremely time consuming. Bolen remembered that they also needed to get in touch with quite a few people to see if anyone had been seen giving medication to John the Tuesday morning of his death. He decided that Saturday and Sunday would be good days to reach the majority of the people. Bolen made plans to leave directions for some of the officers to make the calls and follow up on that information.

I had no plans for Friday night, so I decided to spend the time doing a little research and then maybe curling up with the girls to watch a movie. I had not watched *Casablanca* for a couple of years. That was a mélange of actors in a 1943 movie that eventually became a classic.

I received a call from the brothers. They often called together by putting me on speaker. They thanked me for inviting them to Thanksgiving dinner.

Oliver said, "I know that Mother would want us to be together, but Danica has a lot of family coming to her parents' home, and she is insistent that I need to meet everyone."

William remarked, "Cally's parents will be going out of town, so we will be able to come. Can I bring anything?"

I answered, "Yes, make your crab dip. Everyone will love it." I continued, "Oliver, we will miss you, but I understand."

Next a little research, and then *Casablanca*.

I looked up some more information about Hadrian Rose. It appeared that Rose had been the founder of Equestrian Insurance Company. In his late twenties, he began the company by insuring horses. It had been quite successful, and he had branched out into different kinds of insurance. He founded the company and was also the CEO. The company had been still growing at the time of his death. His son, Hall Rose, assumed the role as CEO after his father's demise. The company was doing well if and when Hadrian committed suicide. It was still listed as a strong and healthy insurance company, so what could it have been that made him choose the particular avenue of suicide?

More research strongly indicated that Hadrian Rose had indeed ended his own life. Why? It appeared his family was devastated. I was curious as to whether or not he had left a note, and how did any of this connect with John George or Robert Goodson? If Rose had a connection to John George, could John have known something about Rose that was so powerful that he would take his own life? Perhaps he could have. I could expect that of John George, but how could that suicide have a connection to the death of John George, when Hadrian Rose was already dead? Maybe it didn't. Maybe it was just a one-way street and nothing more.

I couldn't help being curious about what was found in John George's files. He obviously had not left secret information where it could easily be found. Also I couldn't help wondering who wanted Robert Goodson dead. After what Sandra had said, I could imagine a lot of people would have been happy to see him receive some retribution.

Thinking about the investigation, I knew I had been helpful thus far to the case. I just needed to connect some more of those rascally dots. At that time those dots were all over the place. They reminded me of a glass-enclosed ant farm with the glass broken and the ants running everywhere. I needed to corral them somehow.

Back to Thanksgiving. I knew I could easily seat three more people. I thought about inviting Rory and Shae Campbell from my Sunday school class. Rory was the attorney I had connected Abella with a few months earlier when she desperately needed an attorney. Brad and Abella would be out of town sharing each other with their respective families. With the new business, Amy couldn't get away to Ireland to meet Cian's family, but Cian had purchased tickets for his parents to fly over here. I would invite Rory and Shae.

I called, and, yes, you guessed it, no answer. I left a message for Rory and Shae about Thanksgiving dinner.

Finally on to *Casablanca*. Maybe I would pick up an idea or two from the movie to help me with this John, Robert, Herman, Poor June, Sandra, Hadrian puzzle. Could an ex-freedom fighter who saved his old love and her husband from the Nazis offer me anything to do with the case? It did get him into trouble. There was love. And there was fog. My brain was in a fog with all the twists and turns coming from John George. Could Hadrian Rose have loved someone so much that he ended his life for him, her, or them, rather than to see him, her, or them get hurt? Interesting concept to explore—after the movie.

Bolen called June George to ask her if John had a medication that he used for his migraines. She said that John had found Relpax to work better than some of the other drugs he had tried. Yes, she said, he had begun a migraine the evening before, but he had taken his medicine and it relieved it. That Tuesday morning he had commented at breakfast that the migraine was gone, and she assumed that he had either decided he didn't need the medicine or had forgotten to take it with him. She revealed that there was a filled prescription of the Relpax for John still at their house.

Bolen thanked her for her help. Bolen persistently turned the information around in his head. If John had thought the migraine had gone away Tuesday morning but it continued to bother him, he may have mentioned it to someone at the courthouse and been given medicine from that person. But like Harri had said, who would have known at the courthouse that John would have a migraine and bring something with them that would kill him? Bolen felt like he was getting closer to answers, but some things still were not adding up. "I suppose it always could have been some random stranger just in for the thrill of the kill," he thought.

Monday morning, Bolen discovered that there were two more people yet to be contacted about the medication. He was definitely looking forward to that report. As a detective one could easily grow cynical, but Bolen believed that it helped to try to stay as positive as possible. He thought about the medication. He knew that even if someone did see medication being offered to John, it did not mean it was the medication that killed him. There were many paths to follow. Police had to be willing to search each path. There was a quote by Ralph Marston that Bolen had framed and hung in his office. "There are plenty of difficult obstacles in your path. Don't allow yourself to become one of them." To Bolen that was one of the most important things for a police detective to remember.

Bolen thought about Hadrian Rose. His file was one of the files stolen from John George and discovered in Robert Goodson's office. In the file there was proof that Hadrian's computer had held thousands of inappropriate, unlawful pictures. He must have wiped his computer clean or disposed of it before he killed himself. He killed himself either because he did not want to hurt his family, or as in many cases, his pride in people seeing him as the good man and father in the city could not bear the thought of being seen otherwise. Whatever it was that brought him to the suicide decision, it kept his name pristine in the community and kept him from facing years in a penitentiary. Bolen wondered why that file had been stolen. Robert could not blackmail Hadrian. Had Robert been into blackmail? "I suppose he could try to blackmail someone in the Rose family," Bolen thought. "Perhaps it would be wise to run some telephone numbers against each other, those belonging to Robert Goodson against Hall, who had succeeded his father, and those at Hadrian's home, where the widow still resided with her daughter and son-in-law. It couldn't hurt."

Bolen made arrangements to meet with his union snitch Wednesday morning. The man had intimated that he had pertinent information against Herman Glotz. In the file about Herman that had been discovered in Goodson's office, there were written notes about offenses, but no real evidence of wrongdoing. John had written that he had two people willing to give evidence about Glotz, but he had not named who they were. He must have told Glotz who they were and Glotz must have known they were credible, since he had given John money, according to the money book. If Glotz wasn't guilty of murder—and Bolen was not ruling him out—he probably was guilty of something for which he could be arrested, and with Goodson out of the way, Glotz was looking better and better as a murder suspect.

The union snitch was a strong union man who believed in his union fully; however, he was a man of conscience and wanted to weed out the corruption that seemed to be gathering within his union. To do so he was willing to work with the police under the cover of confidentiality. He also had told Bolen that he held a strong belief that union members should be able to vote, and vote secretly, on decisions regarding where any union monies were given politically, although the issue wasn't a police matter.

I thought Skinny wasn't as grouchy as usual since I had been taking her to work. I decided I would take her at least three or four of the six days I worked. Happy cat meant happier dogs and a happier me. Truthfully I wouldn't go as far as to say happy cat; it was Skinny, after all, but less grouchy cat worked too.

I had proceeded no further with my suspects than a conspiracy that could have included Robert Goodson, Herman Glotz, Sandra Jersey Bachman Goldman, and Poor June George. Where did Hadrian Rose fit in, or did he? I had to keep my mind open to just one murderer, as much as I thought I could see those dots connecting. As I was working and thinking about it, the noon news came on the radio.

Uh oh! Someone had spilled the beans and the newscaster was saying that the Courtroom Poisoner of John George had used a mixture of oxycodone, fentanyl and heroin. I wondered if that was true. If it was, it definitely wasn't any of the poisons I had been researching. It was interesting in that it included a couple of opiods and that was what the court case I had been on was about. Was oxycodone, fentanyl and heroin a strange mixture? I didn't know. I imagined that it could be very lethal. I also wondered who would get into trouble for leaking that information. Someone in the forensics lab, if the person could be discovered, would lose his or her job. I was certainly thankful that I hadn't known and it wasn't me doing the leaking.

Now we needed to discover just how those drugs had been administered. That information likely wasn't known yet by the news media. Probably it wasn't known because I didn't believe the police had that answer yet. Of course the news media was guessing and had "experts" who were giving their ideas as to how the murder may have taken place. There were people out there in the listening world who took ideas, assumptions, and opinions as facts. I researched everything, but I found that even to be challenging lately. There were so many sites that looked factual but weren't, so finding the truth had become considerably more difficult.

In researching I found that fentanyl by itself, even one dose, could be fatal. The heroin-fentanyl mixture was certainly a fatal mixture. I discovered that they both had nonpolar molecules that could penetrate membranes to reach the brain more quickly than many other drugs. Oxycodone was polar but nothing to mess around with either.

It was such a beautiful day that I could hardly wait to get home to take the girls for a walk. We were having a short spell of Indian summer, which according to *The Old Farmer's Almanac* could occur between November eleven and November twenty. I wanted to enjoy every moment of it that I could. I didn't really mind winter weather, but I did love those nice warm days that surprised us in November. The only thing about winter that I did mind were the decreased daylight hours.

We were fast losing the leaves on our trees. When I was a child and my dad raked leaves, he would make a leaf outline of a house for me, filled with leaf-lined rooms inside. That leaf house awakened my imagination, and I could play in it for a couple of hours, if my brothers were busy elsewhere. If not, they thought it was fun to run back and forth through my house to ruin it. I thought my neighbors might question my sanity if I tried making a leaf house now. My dogs, however, loved jumping into a big pile of raked leaves. At least they could have fun and enjoy themselves when I raked, even though I had to rake the pile again before preparing the leaves for composting. Running over them with the lawn mower made them the perfect size for the compost heap.

Our city had just voted in a new mayor. I decided to send her a congratulatory bouquet, which reminded me that I had asked Bolen one day, "If I hadn't sent you a congratulatory bouquet when you were promoted to detective, would you have come by my shop?"

Bolen answered, "I would have, but it may have taken me a couple of months longer to do so." It had been difficult for him to quit blaming himself for not finding me when I had been kidnapped.

Bolen called Sandra Goldman for answers to questions about John apprising her that he had taken medication after arriving at the courthouse the morning that he died. She told him that John had mentioned the migraine and disclosed that he had not been able to find his bottle of migraine pills at his home that morning. He had been hopeful that the migraine from the night before had worn itself out; however, he said that it appeared to be rearing its ugly head again, and becoming even stronger. He stated that he had received some over-the-counter medication from someone and hoped that it would help to, in his words, "keep it at bay." She further stated, when asked, that she had not seen anyone actually give him any medication. She did, however, see that both Herman and Robert had small bottles of acetaminophen, and noted that they each had offered some to John that morning before 8:30.

Bolen considered what Sandra had said. Acetaminophen seemed safe enough, and probably everyone knew what an acetaminophen tablet looked like, so that shouldn't be a problem. Bolen was trying to remember something. What was it? After steadily thinking about it for fifteen minutes, he remembered. A travel-sized container of acetaminophen had been included in the items brought in from Robert Goodson's desk. Bolen called an officer and asked him to retrieve it from the evidence room and run it over to forensics to send to the lab to check the ingredients.

Tuesday morning arrived, and Bolen found the report on his desk from the rest of the telephone calls. It appeared that a couple of other jurors had also seen Robert Goodson and Herman Glotz offer John George acetaminophen before they were called into court at 8:30. One person remembered seeing the law clerk who was acting as bailiff that day, giving acetaminophen to John before 8:30. The person had wanted to ask the law clerk a question and had been standing relatively close to her and John; otherwise, she said, she probably wouldn't have noticed. Bolen had no reason to suspect the law clerk, which may have been why nothing happened between 8:30 and 10:35. She simply must have given him acetaminophen.

One juror remembered John saying to Herman during the 10:15-to-10:30 break, "I think this migraine is getting worse. I'll take a couple of those pills, if you don't mind." He said Herman pulled the acetaminophen bottle from his pocket and poured some into John's hand, saying, "Take at least three, if you want it to be effective." He saw John throw the pills into his mouth, swallow them, and say, "Thanks, Herman." Again, this information did not prove anything. Those pills may have been just what they were purported to be.

Was it strange for three people to be carrying bottles of acetaminophen? Probably not, Bolen thought, although he did think it more likely that women would be carrying bottles in their purses, since there was more room in a purse than men would have in their pockets. Maybe the containers were not bottles but the narrow travel-sized containers that were available to purchase. They were relatively small and not bad for pocket carrying. He believed those usually contained yellow caplets. He decided to have an officer again call the jurors who actually saw the medication, to discern whether or not they could tell the kind of container the medications came from and if they were yellow caplets or blue and green capsules. He thought he might be asking a bit much from their memories, but it was worth a try; however, he wasn't sure at this point that any of it made a real difference.

Bolen decided after he spoke to the union man the next morning that he could begin bringing some of the suspects in for questioning. It could be good; that was, if they did not immediately get a lawyer, because the interrogators would then get nothing. Maybe, instead, he would just drop by to see the people and ask what he hoped would appear to be innocuous questions. Perhaps that would work better. As usual his captain was getting antsy, which never turned out to be a good thing.

Bolen gave me a call. He asked if I'd like to go to dinner Wednesday night and maybe then watch the 2018 *Overboard* that had been put on hold.

"That sounds great," I answered. "I enjoy something to look forward to that breaks up the work week."

"What if I pick you up at your house at six o'clock?" Bolen asked. "Is that okay?"

"That works," I answered.

Before leaving work Tuesday evening, Bolen received the comparable report on telephone numbers between the Roses and Robert Goodson that he had previously requested. There were not any calls between any of their numbers. That fact nearly excluded the Roses from having received threats of blackmail from Goodson. If they had not been blackmailed, then why would they kill him? He wasn't the one who had blackmailed Hadrian Rose, and it did not appear that the family knew anything about John George and his blackmail. Why then had Robert Goodson stolen Hadrian's file? Maybe he planned to use blackmail but had not yet put his plan into action. But it was strange that he had not stolen any of the other one hundred files he could have easily stolen if he was planning to use blackmail. None of this information was coming together with the Hadrian connection, but Bolen felt that a connection existed. It simply had not been uncovered yet.

The meeting with the union man went exceedingly well for Bolen. The information he received was even better than expected. He was given specific evidence proving corruption in the union by the two top men holding offices. In addition he had evidence to substantiate that those same two men were giving union money to Herman Glotz, who had uncovered their nefarious enterprises. The evidence was overwhelming and would prove to make open-and-shut cases. Bolen had the evidence, but he didn't want to use it yet, because he wanted to get Glotz first on the murder charge, if that proved possible. What was the missing link or who was the missing link who could give the needed evidence for the murder? He was almost certain that the same person who killed John George had killed Robert Goodson.

The dogs received a half-hour walk and got to play outside while I readied myself to go out to dinner. I had the five o'clock news on as background noise. Someone had discovered that Goodson had been on the same jury with John George, and the news media was connecting the dots of those two murders and commenting that the murders had to be related. They did not know how, but said they would be investigating. Did we actually have any investigative reporters in our city? I supposed we had some wannabes. They had to start somewhere.

On the way home from work, I had stopped at Pie in the Sky and picked up dessert for Bolen and me. We could enjoy it while we watched the movie.

Bolen arrived to pick me up at one minute before six. We went to a restaurant called Cibo Ottimo that was new to me. It was Italian, which was my favorite food. That reminded me I had eaten my very favorite Italian food in Atlanta, Georgia. I had enjoyed my favorite German food and favorite Cuban food in Florida. I had eaten my favorite Greek dish in Pennsylvania. The best biscuits I had ever eaten were found in Memphis, Tennessee, as well as the best-tasting ice cream. There was an Indian restaurant in Colorado that made tremendous fruited naan. For the best fried okra at a restaurant, it was in Ooltewah, Tennessee. Their pies and meatloaf were pretty great too. My friend from India, who lives in Texas, made the most terrific *dosas* and you couldn't find curry like hers anywhere other than her house. Yummy!

"Harri, are you with me?" Bolen asked.

"So sorry!" I exclaimed. "I was getting a good start on food hopping around the United States. Don't ask. It's not worth repeating aloud."

"At least you're back from your journey," Bolen kidded. "Are you tired now?" he asked, laughing.

"Okay, I deserve a little mocking. I admit it," I commented. "But it was fun while it lasted, remembering all of those scrumptious flavors. But I'm looking forward to some great flavors tonight. Everything on this menu looks good."

"I've eaten here only two other times," Bolen said, "but I thoroughly enjoyed each of those meals. I especially like their osso buco."

"I think I'll try the lemo, aglio, parmigiano paste con carciofo e gamberetto," I announced to the waiter. "That sounds remarkable."

"I have some interesting news," Bolen offered. "In following up on some leads about the John George case, we have discovered other crimes for which people will be arrested. That includes one of our suspects; however, I want to get the murder solved first. If this suspect is guilty of murder, I want that crime to be tried before the other lesser ones."

"I can understand that," I stated. "I haven't come up with any new ideas, although there is still something that my brain is trying to bring to the forefront that has remained elusive."

Bolen said, "I believe there is one thing or one person who holds the key to this whole thing, for both murders, but as yet I do not know what or who it is. Right now I still don't know if there is one murderer or if this was indeed a conspiracy. From some of the information coming in, I am strongly leaning toward a conspiracy, but we are still trying to get more evidence."

Bolen's phone rang. He answered the call. After he was finished he disclosed, "I'm afraid after we eat that I will need to get back to the department. We just received some evidentiary information that calls for further action. I'm truly sorry. We'll have to postpone our movie for another evening."

"That is definitely more important than movie watching," I commented. "We can even do takeout if you want, and I can take a taxi home."

"I'll take you home, but if you don't mind, let's do takeout. I can eat at the police department," Bolen shared. "You are a real trooper, Harri Bedlington. I don't think I've ever known anyone quite like you. Thanks."

"Hey, it just makes sense," I said. "I want you to solve this murder almost as much as you do. I need to get my mind back on things like floral displays and wedding decorations instead of murders," I said drolly.

Bolen called the waiter over and told him that we needed to make our order a takeout. The waiter said he would take care of it. Before long he brought our food to us, and we were good to go. It smelled wonderful. I noticed that Bolen left a tip for the waiter, which was thoughtful, since we hadn't eaten our meal there. Little things like that were important.

Bolen dropped me at home and headed for the police department.

The lab report was in and the acetaminophen bottle from Robert Goodson's office had contained the acetaminophen capsules but they were filled with fentanyl, heroin, and oxycodone. This forensic information meant that Goodson definitely had something to do with the murder. Either he gave John George the fatal dose and/or he was part of the conspiracy since Glotz had been seen giving acetaminophen to John. Bolen decided he would need to get a warrant to search Herman Glotz's office and home for the same pills; however, if Herman was smarter than Goodson, he would have rid himself of the drugs. Bolen thought he had to go for it, though, since Glotz was seen giving medicine to John.

As Bolen walked into his office area, another detective said, "We have a rather strange coincidence going on. A homeless man who was also a veteran died a few days ago. His labs came back saying it was fentanyl, heroin, and oxycodone that caused the fatality. In the report it stated that his friend told the doctor and the officer on call that the man had simply taken a couple of acetaminophen capsules. The man's backpack is still in evidence. I checked it, and it contained an acetaminophen bottle. I sent it to forensics for prints."

"Wow!" exclaimed Bolen. "It sounds like things are really beginning to take off. I believe I will add getting Glotz's prints to the search warrant. It could prove useful. Then we will know whether or not he killed Goodson. Wait, did the report on the homeless victim say where he had found the acetaminophen bottle?"

"A courthouse dumpster," answered the detective.

Information was coming in fast at that point, Bolen

thought. He wrote out the Glotz warrant and had it attested to. He wanted to get the searches started bright and early the next morning, so he was going to take the chance of bothering a judge. First he'd have an officer find out if any judges were working late, because it didn't seem quite as bad to bother someone working late as to bother a judge who was at home or who had gone out for the evening.

One of the officers ran the warrant over to the courthouse. He was fortunate. A judge was in the process of closing up his office and was in a good mood, since he was through with work for the evening and was heading home. He read the warrant, asked a few pertinent questions and then signed it.

The search had nothing to do with the union blackmail. It was strictly for discovering medication and any papers, emails, or text messages alluding either to being on the jury, the murder or to the drugs that killed John George and evidently also a homeless veteran.

The next morning the police arrived at the Glotz home at 5:30. Glotz was immediately taken to the police station to obtain his fingerprints, and then he was returned to his home. He was free to stay there or go to his office, which the police were also searching. Glotz chose to get into his car and drive to his office where he parked his car and remained in it until the police were through with the search.

It was discovered that Glotz had two phones. One appeared to be his phone for home and business. The other phone was a disposable phone often called a throwaway or burner. On that phone there were only three numbers for which he had placed calls and from which he had received calls. Someone got to work immediately making calls to those numbers. One was answered by a police detective. It proved to be one of Goodson's telephones. The other two were answered by two different women, both of whom immediately ended the calls when they discovered it was not Glotz on the other end of the line. That was an interesting turn of events. Who were those women? The only women closely looked at had been Sandra and June, thought Bolen. Whoever had those phones would most likely get rid of them quickly. There wasn't enough evidence to get a warrant for a search. Of course it may not have been Sandra or June who answered the phones. It was a problem; the police did not know who the women were.

As time wore on, information came in on the fingerprint analysis of the acetaminophen bottle found in the homeless man's backpack. Besides those of the homeless man, another fingerprint matched one that the police already had on file. It was the same print as that found on the poker that killed Robert Goodson, which meant that the person who killed Robert Goodson was also in on the murder of John George. "We can only hope that it turns out to be Glotz," ruminated Bolen, as they had Glotz's fingerprints by then. Bolen called Lily Forager in forensics and asked her to have someone compare Glotz's fingerprints to the department's unknown print.

"Hey, Bolen," Lily said. "I'll be happy to do that. How are you doing? I haven't seen much of you lately. You ever see that girl we worked with named Harri? She was a fun one, wasn't she?"

"As a matter of fact, Lily, I see her fairly often. I know your technique. You're trying your best to learn the answer to the latest gossip about me right from the horse's mouth, as they say," Bolen commented. "The truth is she is fun. I see her and talk to her often. We're friends. Does that satisfy your curiosity?"

"Nearly," answered Lily, chuckling a bit.

"Hey, I appreciate that you will try to match that print for me," Bolen imparted. "It won't exclude a murderer if the prints are not his, but if they are his, it will be evidence that he definitely is a murderer."

Only one more week until Thanksgiving. I knew I quickly had to make a list of everything I needed to buy and do to get ready. My mother was very organized and a great list-maker. I didn't make them often enough, but when I had something scheduled like serving eleven people for Thanksgiving, I absolutely had to make a list and check off each thing as it was accomplished. I'm more of a fly-by-the-seat-of-my-pants person otherwise. I needed to clean, decorate, buy food, fix food, etc. My list, however, would be very detailed, down to every last thing, probably even to washing my hair, just to make sure every time slot was allotted.

People wanted Thanksgiving arrangements for their homes, which usually meant a hefty work week. I knew the good news for those of us working as florists would be if everyone ordered early, so we wouldn't have to work late Wednesday on arrangements for Thursday and Friday. I never counted on it though.

When it came to cooking for Thanksgiving, I had a new potato ricer to try for making mashed potatoes. I purchased it hoping it would help reduce the lumps. I always managed to have lumps in my mashed potatoes. My brothers always said they liked them that way (kudos to my brothers). My mother never had lumps in her mashed potatoes. Somehow I had missed that lesson. I had missed all of the cooking lessons. It's probably amazing that I learned how to cook at all.

On Monday morning Bolen received the report comparing Glotz's fingerprints with the unknown prints. Glotz's prints did not match the print from the acetaminophen bottle or the poker. Bolen had been hopeful that there would be a match but knew that in police work, it was always two steps forward and one step back. In fact often it seemed more like three steps back. The information technology people were still going through Glotz's computers, iPad, and phones. Something could still turn up. It was slow going because many people who worked for the police department were taking vacations that Thanksgiving week.

Some news came in to Bolen about a text discovered on Robert Goodson's phone that had been sent to him a few months before telling him to set his jury duty for the last week in October. That information had come from one of the throwaway phones numbers previously discovered. That news was interesting. Someone knew that Goodson had received a summons to jury but was deferring it, and that person was giving Goodson the date to defer it to, definitely lending credence to the conspiracy theory. Wait a minute. The text he received was a group text and was also sent to two other numbers. One went to an unknown number that the police had discovered, and one went to Glotz's disposable phone. There was no longer any doubt about a conspiracy. None whatsoever. It would be great evidence for showing a conspiracy, and at least the police finally had some proof that Glotz was in on it.

Bolen was almost sure that one of the three people still alive who was involved in that four-way text had also killed Goodson. Glotz had been cleared of the Goodson murder, which left the two anonymous phone numbers. Bolen knew that women had those phones because of the phone calls the police made to those numbers. Discerning which women were in on the conspiracy would be the clincher. The fact that Bolen knew of two female suspects did not mean they were the women in on the conspiracy. It could be two other women who were being blackmailed that the police had not yet connected to the murder. Bolen asked himself, "How are we to find these women? I'd like to find them before arresting Glotz."

Before leaving work for the day, Bolen left word for someone to those two anonymous phone numbers to see who else, if anyone, had been called from the disposable phones. He continued thinking, if those texts had been sent four months ago, John George's murder was an extremely well-planned, premeditated murder. But how could they have planned for the migraine? Bolen could not come up with an answer to that question. Actually there were more questions than answers. How in the world did they all get on the same jury? I suppose if they were all called to that courtroom, it could happen, but the odds of it happening must surely have been infinitesimal. Did the murderers just hope that they would run into him after all of that planning? How did it happen? It seemed to be one of those so-close-and-yet-so-far situations. The closer he got, the more questions arose taking him further in another direction.

That night Bolen called me at 9:00 on his way home from work and asked if he could come by for a few minutes to run some questions by me that he had about the case. He said that bouncing them off someone might help him come up with some answers since he had been going over and over them in his mind but wasn't getting anywhere.

I told him, "Sure. Come ahead. I'll try to keep quiet."

Bolen came and we went over and over his questions. I remained mostly silent, believe it or not, except every once in a while, I made a little noise to let him know that I was still listening. After a while he said, "It's not working. I appreciate your listening, but I don't seem to be making any headway."

"Listen," I said, "let me ask you some questions, okay?"

"Of course. Go ahead," Bolen responded.

"Three people got that group text about setting the jury duty for the last week of October. Is that correct?" I asked.

"Yes," Bolen answered.

"We know that Goodson and Glotz received the texts," I stated. "We don't know who the other person was who received the text, nor do we know who sent the text. Is that also correct?"

"Yes," Bolen answered again.

"Okay," I commented. "The people who received the

texts were evidently supposed to send in change of jury dates to get on jury duty the same time as John George. That had to be why they were sent the texts. Do you agree to that?"

"Yes, I do," Bolen responded.

"Then someone knew when John was going to be on jury duty, as he himself must have deferred his original time and reset the time he would be able to go. John must have told someone. He could have told any or all of those people, but then why send the text? Those people had in some way talked and discovered that they each had been summoned to court. I know when I received my summons that I mentioned it to several people. That's not an unusual thing to do. I also deferred my going until the last week of October. Oh, that could make me a suspect, couldn't it? But to continue, if all of that happened, who would be the most likely person to know when John was going to court? It obviously wasn't any of those three, because they were sent the information so that they could make their plans. I think the finger of destiny is pointing at none other than Poor June."

"You are so right," declared Bolen. "This is all conjecture without any evidence against June, but it does make sense. She either already knew those people or found out that John was blackmailing them, and it would make sense that they would want John out of the way, so she contacted them and they formed a sweet little conspiracy."

"I think those people had already met," I said, "or at least been in touch with each other about murdering John. They probably had been looking for what they considered the perfect way to commit the crime without anyone being able to figure out who committed it. When they mentioned their summons to jury duty to Ms. Anonymous Number One, who I believe to be Poor June, she must have figured that would be the way to go, after John also received a summons. The rest of the group must have agreed with her. The good news about all of this was that Robert Goodson forgot to remove the information about the October date from his texts."

"Thanks, Harri," Bolen said. "I now, at least, have an answer to one of my questions, and that is immensely helpful. If I don't get answers from somewhere else soon, we'll have to do this again to see if we can come up with another answer."

"Anytime," I answered. "I'm just pleased that I could be of some help. I'll keep my mind churning on those other questions too. Did I tell you I'm looking to have dinner ready about two o'clock on Thursday?"

"No," Bolen said, "but that's fine for me. As a matter of fact I can come by early if you want me to and help out. My mother taught me to be helpful in the kitchen."

"That sounds great," I responded. "Kudos to your mother. Anyway, I always wanted a sous chef. You want to come around noon?"

"That works for me," Bolen answered. "I'd better take off now. Thanks for listening and for your insight. I'll see you Thursday."

Bolen and I had talked for at least an hour. In trying to answer Bolen's questions I had become so fired up that I knew sleep was out of the way for a while. I decided to get ready for bed and get a good start on my latest book. I was going to read *Kidnapped* by Robert Louis Stevenson. It was definitely a change from *The Idiot,* which I had recently finished. You also may be wondering why in the world only a couple years after my own kidnapping I would dare read a book called *Kidnapped.* I believed in facing my fears head on, to get rid of them, and part of me was hopeful that the book would be very different from my own experience. Besides, it was on my reading list, and I was determined to read it.

Wednesday morning seemed to come earlier than usual. I had stayed up longer than I should have while reading, but it had taken me the extended time to get sleepy. I had a long and busy day ahead of me. I was very thankful, however, that I did not have a Thanksgiving vacation wedding that weekend. I knew I would be busy enough as it was. Every evening after work for the previous week I had either shopped or cleaned. The previous night before Bolen came by, I had decorated. Hey, why be a florist if you can't make something beautiful for yourself once in a while? My table was all set, and I thought it looked absolutely fabulous. All the other rooms were cleaned and ready to go too. My guest bathroom was spotless and decorated. It didn't get a lot of use, so it was easy to clean. I was thankful that my parents had gifted me with their china when they moved. There were place settings for fifteen people. That particular set had been passed down from my great grandparents, so it had a special meaning to me. Before I received it, I had planned to buy twelve different place settings for an unusual-looking table. I still may do that someday. I'd have to hit some estate sales, garage sales, thrift stores, and even antique shops. Someday.

I did not get home until 9:15 Wednesday night. I was so tired that I went right to bed. Well, I almost went right to bed. First I gave some treats to my dogs that had let me know in no uncertain terms that they felt I had neglected them, even though William had come by earlier to feed them. I put them outside while I removed the giblets from the turkey. The giblets would be used the next day for making the broth that would go into the dressing. I would be getting up early to get that huge turkey in the oven so that it had time to cook long enough, but also so that I would have time to take the turkey out to get some good juices for the gravy. I had a great and easy recipe for roasting a turkey that did not require basting, yet it always came out very moist.

Thursday morning arrived. It promised to be a beautiful day, but was still dark when I arose. I had cleaned the turkey and prepared it for roasting, and I managed to get it in the oven. I had placed the giblets in a pan of water with diced celery and onions and various spices, and it was simmering. I had minced fresh oranges and cranberries for a salad. Most of the items that would go into the dressing were prepared, ready and waiting to be mixed together before being placed in the oven. I still had to rice the potatoes.

Darla and Lucas were bringing Darla's grandmother's recipe of southern sweet potatoes with brown sugar and pecans. Adelyn and Gabriel were bringing a relish plate. Shae and Rory were bringing a green bean casserole. William was bringing his crab dip. Cally had insisted on bringing something too, and I think she said a bean salad. My grandmother used to make one. I wondered if it was the same. Florence was bringing two chocolate pies and two coconut cream pies, all four with meringue. Bolen was bringing roasted cauliflower with an herb-caper sauce. I'm sure you wish you were filling up that twelfth chair that was going to sit empty around my table. Am I right? Does it sound like a lot of starch to you? You may remember that when I was young we lived in the south. We always fixed dressing and two kinds of potatoes. Then we would have added macaroni and cheese to the mix as well. It's Thanksgiving. Let's be thankful. Oh, and did you remember to donate to the rescue mission?

Bolen arrived. I had to taste his cauliflower dish. Oh my, was it ever delicious! He washed his hands and said, "Tell me what you need for me to do, and I'll get to it."

What a help Bolen was! I was thrilled when he offered to take that twenty-five-pound turkey out of the oven for me. I'd had visions of spilling that wonderful broth as well as the turkey all over the kitchen floor. I put him in charge of stirring the gravy until it thickened. After that he carved the turkey and placed the pieces on my large turkey platter. We finished with the food preparation by

1:45, and the last guest had arrived by 1:55. We placed all of the food on the kitchen island, and after Rory blessed our food, I asked my guests to pick up a plate from the table and help themselves to the food.

What a great time we had! I had placed Cally next to me at the table so I had a chance to talk with her. She was a very likable young woman. It was a great group. Everyone talked and laughed. I could tell that Florence was enjoying herself. All the guests made a point of talking with her. I loved that they did that. I was surely fortunate with my friends.

I mentioned my book list, and several people began talking about the books they loved or the books they were reading. Shae shared that she had just begun to read *To Kill A Mockingbird*. She added, "I wonder if I'll find similarities of Atticus Finch in Rory. It is the first book I've read that deals with a lawyer since Rory and I were married."

My mind went to remember who had written the book. It was Harper Lee. Some people even questioned if she had written it or if her sister had written it. At that moment the thing that had been niggling at me for a couple of weeks hit me. "Bolen," I shouted. All twenty eyes looked at me. I must have sounded shocking to them. "Bolen," I said again, "Harper."

"Yes?" Bolen asked. "What about Harper?"

"Maybe I should tell you in private," I said. "It has to do with your case."

"Sure," Bolen said. "Will you all excuse us for just a moment, please?"

I led Bolen back to the guest bedroom. Once in I said, "The thing that I have been trying to think of for two weeks came to my mind when Shae talked about reading *To Kill A Mockingbird*. It was written by Harper Lee."

"Yes, I am aware that Harper Lee was the author," Bolen responded. "How does this fit into my case?" he asked.

I realized that I had not explained myself well at all. "Okay," I said. "Here it is. I read Hadrian Rose's obituary some time ago. He had a daughter named Harper. That is the part I was trying to remember and connect those dots."

"And?" Bolen asked.

"And, the law clerk slash bailiff during the last day on our court case was named Harper," I added. "It may not be the same person, but Harper is not the most common name. I think it is something to check on. That's all."

"Harri," Bolen said, "I think you are right. That may just be the link I have been searching for. We checked out Hall, Hadrian's son, and even Hadrian's widow. We did not look into phone calls specifically to Hadrian's daughter. We evidently assumed she would be covered by the widow's phone since she and her husband were living there with her. We should have caught that fact and checked her out, even if she proved not to be involved. It was very poor policing. Thanks. You are wonderful." Bolen pulled me close and gave me the first twenty-second kiss I had received from him.

"I think I need another epiphany," I declared, "if it means I get one of those kisses with it every time."

The other nine people shouted saying, "You have been away from the table long enough." "What's going on in there?"

Rory said, "We're ready for Miss Florence's delicious looking desserts."

I knew I was probably flushed when I headed out of the bedroom and toward the table.

William asked, "Are you sure that was all about the case?"

Darla said, "Shame on you, William! Leave your poor sister alone, or we'll never get our dessert."

Bolen helped me pick up everyone's plates. We put away all the leftover food that needed refrigeration and cleaned off the island. Next we placed the pies on the island and cut them. I made a pot of coffee and put cups, cream, chocolate powder, and cinnamon beside the coffeepot. I told everyone to come and get it. They needed to stretch their legs anyway, I told them. I knew those pies would be gone in no time, and I was right. There was hardly a crumb left.

After dessert we convened in my great room and continued talking. Florence said she thought she should go home; turkey always made her sleepy. We all thanked her for coming and for bringing her pies. Bolen walked her home carrying her empty pie plates for her.

I asked everyone what they were especially grateful for that year. No one said anything, so I began, "I am thankful for my new business, my new friends, my old friends, my church, and my family." That comment got the others started with what they were grateful for. It was a great way to end a wonderful day.

About an hour later, everyone else began to leave. I gave the plates and bowls back to the people who had brought food along with a take-home package of turkey. By the time the last person, minus Bolen, had gone, I was feeling that the tryptophan in the turkey was catching up to me too. Of course the sleepiness most likely was from too much starchy food, the long, busy morning I had experienced and that this introvert had been extroverting for several hours.

Bolen expressed, "You look like you're going to fall asleep standing there. Why don't you go take a nap? I'll take the dogs out in back and play with them for a while before I go home."

"I'll take you up on that. Thanks," I said, and gave him a hug.

I actually slept for three hours. I had needed that nap. When I got up, the dogs were all sleeping on their beds. It was already dark outside. I walked through the house to finish cleaning up only to discover that all the work was done. The china had been hand-washed and dried. The rest was in the dishwasher, which had already gone through all of its cycles. The table was back in place, and the tablecloth was on top of the washing machine.

I called Bolen to thank him. I did not reach him. He was either working or napping himself. I hoped he was napping, so I texted him my thanks. His surprise with the clean-up was nearly the best I had ever received. It was just so thoughtful.

I lounged on my couch. Why did one piece of furniture have so many names? Couch, sofa, divan, davenport, even settee? I never knew which to call it. People from some areas of the country called it one thing, others another. It was kind of like the pop, soda, Coke, soft drink predilection. What you called your carbonated drink appeared to depend on the part of the country where you lived. I conjectured that the onset of television probably had brought more unity throughout the states in speech, including the various accents, than had been seen before. Also, since that time period, more people had been on the move, taking jobs across the country; however, there definitely were still some differences to be found among the people of the fifty states. It could be an interesting study. I was sure someone had written about it.

I thought about Harper. I didn't want to get her into trouble. She had seemed to be a nice person. I didn't know her last name, so she might just be that, a nice person; however, what if she were in on the conspiracy? I saw many ways that she could have been involved, such as with the drugs or even in some way with jury tampering. I wondered if her involvement could cause the verdict we had given to be overturned. I did not think the prosecutor would want to retry that case, since the evidence had not been there to support a guilty verdict. I didn't know for sure, though. Strange things did happen. I hoped he wouldn't retry it. Even if there was tampering, it wasn't done for the purpose of changing the case outcome where our jury had been obliged to determine guilt or no guilt. Any tampering happened for the purpose of murdering John George. That physician, the defendant, had been through enough already. I hoped he was allowed to get his medical license unsuspended, since he had been declared not guilty.

What about Poor June? Other than a phone number that had sent a text to the other three involved, there was no evidence against her that I was aware of, and if they could not find the phone and know who it belonged to, it was not even evidence. I foresaw that there still was a long way to go to solve the case. The police certainly could have used a break.

I also saw that I was getting nowhere. It was as if all the dots had disappeared, except for Herman Glotz. The only evidence was the text he received. It was all blank paper. Someone needed to shake the red plastic-framed child's drawing toy and get those dots back into place.

Friday arrived, and it was hazy with rain in the forecast. It was also the day people called Black Friday, which was a big day for shopping. Other than traffic, I did not expect it to affect me much. I had not advertised any sales; therefore, if more shoppers dropped in, it would simply be because they were in our area. I did have a lot of work, and Adelyn had the day off. I had several large floral arrangements to make, as there were many holiday parties taking place that evening and Saturday. We would soon be hitting another busy time of year with holiday weddings and many more holiday parties. Thankfully I had worked in the industry long enough to have an idea of what to expect before opening my own florist shop.

Bolen had reached his home Thanksgiving night at about 7:30 and was in bed by 8:00. He arrived at work quite early Friday morning, met with his team, and shared with them about Harper Rose Lewis. He also asked his team members for input on how they thought the investigation should proceed. After the meeting he knocked on his captain's door. He was invited in. Bolen shared with him exactly where the investigators were in the two cases and the ideas he and his team had put forth. Bolen and the team had made the decision to speak with each of the three suspects, as they had not been questioned a second time when they questioned some of the jurors a second time. There was not enough evidence to bring the suspects in under arrest, and the police did not want the suspects hiring attorneys at that point. Harper, however, was a lawyer, which could work to her benefit. Sometimes it worked as a detriment, because there were attorneys who thought they knew how to answer questions and assumed themselves smarter than the detectives. The detectives knew it worked to their own benefit to let suspects think that way. The captain agreed with Bolen.

Before leaving the precinct, Bolen noticed a report on his desk about the anonymous disposable telephones. There had been other calls that had been made from two of the phones. The one that had sent the text to the other three, which could possibly belong to June George, had several calls to Mary Dee's Hair Salon, one call to the All-American Cable Company, and two calls to England's National Rose Tea Shoppe. The anonymous disposable phone that had received the text had made only one call to a number other than Goodson's, Glotz's, or the first phone. That telephone had placed a call to the City Symphony and Opera office.

Bolen took the report to an officer on his team and asked, "Will you check out these places and try to discover any connections from those telephone calls to our suspects?"

Bolen and two other detectives began their questioning with June George. They apprised her that they were questioning jurors and also had some follow-up questions for her. They disclosed to her that some of the jurors had seen John taking acetaminophen from certain people while in the courthouse. They shared that information with her to see if she would contact the others involved to warn them that the police were questioning the giving of acetaminophen. They also asked her if she had ever had the medications fentanyl and oxycodone in her home.

June was quite cool in answering. "I'm sure I have had those medications, detective," she responded. "I have been through various surgical procedures, and they always sent me home with one or another pain medication. I used them as prescribed. I didn't often have any left over. I had to hide them from John, though, because he would abuse them. And before you ask, since I saw the news report, I have never had heroin in my home. In addition, I do not at this time have any of the oxycodone or fentanyl left from a previous surgery."

Bolen thanked her for her help in the matter. He then asked, "Do you have any questions or any other information that you have thought of that you would like to share with us?"

June responded, "I don't know everything that John was involved in, but perhaps he had people who were unhappy with him. I imagine you've seen his Facebook page. The only question I have is, do you think John could have overdosed? As I mentioned before, it happened more than once."

"We are keeping an open mind about everything, Mrs. George. Anything is possible. Thank you again for being so willing to talk with us. Everything we learn has the possibility of helping bring this terrible matter to a close for you," Bolen stated.

After leaving, Bolen and the other two detectives discussed their time with June. Bolen expressed to them, "It seemed to me that she was trying to point us toward other people as suspects as well as look at John himself. She doesn't know that we confiscated Robert Goodson's acetaminophen bottle that contained the oxycodone, fentanyl and heroin capsules. Neither does she know that another bottle was discovered with the same drugs in them with fingerprints by the person who killed Robert Goodson. There is always the possibility that she could have been trying to help us. On the other hand, I think she was simply trying to mislead us."

The other detectives agreed with Bolen's speculations.

The decision was made to wait two days, which would be Monday, before calling on Herman Glotz to see if June had taken steps to warn the other two suspects. The police would be checking telephone records from June's phones as well as from the other unknown phone. The police had Glotz's disposable phone, so June would have to contact him at one of his other numbers. For all Bolen knew, she would use a pay phone, but as he liked to say, "It's worth a try."

Bolen and his team returned to the police department. Bolen wrote on the white board so they could review the case: 1) Robert Goodson had an acetaminophen bottle with capsules inside containing the drugs that were given to John George. 2) Robert Goodson's murderer also had an acetaminophen bottle with capsules inside containing the drugs that were given to John George. The capsules from this bottle had also killed a homeless veteran. 3) Robert Goodson, Herman Glotz, and Robert Goodson's alleged murderer all received texts about when to sign up for jury duty. 4) If Harper Rose Lewis was on receiving end of that text, she needed to make sure John, Robert, and Herman were called to her courtroom. Placing them in the first of the line, it almost assured a place on the jury. 5) June George was *most likely* the one who sent the texts to the other three.

Bolen continued thinking, "Why would Harper Rose

Lewis want John George murdered? There was no file found on Harper, nor was she mentioned in Hadrian Rose's file that John had amassed and Robert Goodson had stolen. Harper must have discovered that John had been blackmailing her father. She may or may not have known the reason why. If Harper was in any way involved she must have loved her father very much. If she participated, she must have wanted to exact retribution from the man she believed caused her father's death; that is, if the murderer proved to be her. Although Bolen as a rule did not believe in coincidences, he knew there was always that possibility. Harper Rose Lewis could be completely innocent.

Toward late afternoon, Bolen called me and said, "I saw your text this morning. I believe I was already in bed when you sent it last night. I was pleased to be able to help a little. You had spent hours on your feet before I even arrived. How are you today?"

"Thanks to you, all I had to do was wake up from my nap and think about going back to bed," I told Bolen, "although I must admit that I did some thinking about your cases while I was still up. I should have said awake, instead of up, as I was lounging on my sofa. Here's an idea that came to me today while I was working. Check John George's medical records to see if he has ever listed an allergy. If so, get back to me and say yes or no as I understand because of HIPPA that you can't share his records with me. I will tell you what the method to my madness is. Deal?"

"That should be easy enough to do," Bolen stated. "We had to have all of that information from his doctors to study when the autopsy was performed to make sure he had not died of something he was predisposed to. Deal it is. I will look forward to hearing your reasoning."

"Thanks for that, for understanding that I actually do have a reason," I informed him. "You're a chill guy. I've a few more arrangements to put together before going home tonight, so I'd better get to work. I'll have to invest in a headset so I can talk and work at the same time."

"Then everyone who sees you will think you have a

drive-up window," Bolen declared. "Get those pre-made arrangements going for your drive-up business."

"Hey, Bolen," I said, laughing, "I think you may have something there. Maybe I'll hire you for my marketing manager."

"I can't catch you off guard with anything, can I?" Bolen asked.

"Well, that kiss yesterday almost did," I answered.

"Did it really?" Bolen asked. "That's good to know."

"You forgot that I used the word, *almost*," I responded. "If you miss out on things like that, I'm not sure I can hire you as my marketing manager. I may have to put an ad in the paper for someone else to apply for that job."

"Here I was already writing my letter of resignation to the captain so that I could take your job, and you rescind the offer," Bolen proclaimed. "The lady gives and she takes away."

"Absolutely!" I exclaimed. "My prerogative."

"Don't I remember that you have work to do? Snow to shovel or something you mentioned?" Bolen asked.

"Thanks for the reminder," I commented. "I had gotten off track. You don't play fair. You know my mind loves to go on wild rides."

"Ah, now it's the *you-don't-play-fair* routine," Bolen remarked. "Get busy, girl. Get your work done. Then we'll see who plays fair and who doesn't." Bolen was laughing with every word he said.

"Hey, Bolen, thanks for calling. I needed some fun in my day," I said.

"Okay. TTYL," Bolen said and ended the call still laughing.

"What a guy!" I said to myself. "I could get used to having him around."

I finished my work about 8:30 and headed home.

Saturday morning Bolen discovered another report on his desk. It pertained to the telephone numbers of the two unknown disposable telephones. Two of the numbers were businesses that simply could not be of any help. The hair salon number actually was a place that June George had frequented. The officer had written that Harper Rose

Lewis and her husband were donors to the symphony. The symphony secretary, however, had been very pleased to tell the officer that, "Mrs. Lewis was *very friendly* with the maestro and often called him." Again Bolen realized that all these things were circumstantial at best. He hoped they would, though, be useful evidence to use once the police had some direct evidence.

There was also a follow-up report on the capsules in the two acetaminophen bottles that had been discovered. There were no fingerprints on any of the capsules. It had been a long shot, but Bolen knew it had been necessary to check.

Who would the police go to visit on Monday, Bolen wondered. Glotz or Harper Rose Lewis? Since the police had already bothered Glotz once with the search warrants and he had been belligerent then, he was sure to be belligerent about another visit. Bolen decided that visiting Harper Rose Lewis would be the best way to go, and he would try to retrieve her fingerprints in the process. In addition he was hopeful there would have been a telephone call or text to show that June George had tried to warn Glotz and Harper, or whoever the other person was, about the police visit to her at her home.

Bolen showed up in my Sunday school class. He had visited once before, but it had been a quite a while ago. After church Bolen asked if I wanted to go to lunch. I told him, "I have twelve cabbage rolls filled with ground beef, rice, and onions in my slow cooker, covered in a great sauce. If that interests you, come on over to my house." That made me think of an old song I had heard my grandmother play, *Come On-A My House*, circa 1951 sung by Rosemary Clooney. That was so totally different from songs we had now, I thought.

Bolen cleared his throat and said, "Harri?"

I smiled at him. I needn't tell him where my mind had been. "So are you coming?"

With his crooked grin he answered, "That's the best offer I've had today. Of course I'm coming."

"All righty, then," I stated. "I'll meet you at home."

As we were eating I asked, "Have you checked John George's medical records yet for allergies?"

"I must admit that I have not," responded Bolen, "but I do have it written down on my to-do list."

"That question includes all types of allergies or sensitivities, not just to medicines," I enlightened him.

"If tomorrow isn't too busy, I'll check into it," Bolen expressed.

"Just so you know, I have a good reason for asking. The response could prove an answer to one of your questions in the John George case," I explained.

"Okay, I'll check for that information first thing in the morning and call you after checking. I'll try to hold off until six thirty to call you," Bolen said, "but I can't wait any longer than that, because we have to leave before seven to see a suspect."

"You can call me any time after six," I told him. "I will be out of the shower by then."

"By the way, I told my family that you hosted me for Thanksgiving, and my mother said that she wanted me to invite you to their home for Christmas dinner," Bolen relayed.

"How very nice of her," I expressed. "My brothers have already informed me that they have plans for Christmas. So, is it just me, or are you invited too?" I asked, laughing.

"Yes, I'll be there too. It may be a full household, though, with little ones running around everywhere making noise," Bolen said.

"Are you trying to scare me away?" I asked, laughing.

"No, I just want you to be aware of what you may be in for," Bolen said, smiling. "I'd actually like you to meet my family."

At 5:00 Monday morning, Bolen did as he said he would and pulled out John George's medical records. He searched through the reports from all of John's various physicians, writing down everything that looked to him like an allergy or sensitivity as he went through the medical records. He noticed that John was allergic to sulfa, and in searching, discovered a couple of his other medications mentioned that contained sulfa. The doctor had noted that some sulfonamide medications could possibly be okay to take, such as certain anti-inflammatory drugs and even a couple of the migraine medications; however, they were listed as possible allergens so that the doctor would be sure to have the patient watch for reactions in case he needed to take them. Bolen thought, "I wonder what Harri was interested in? I discovered he had allergies to sulfa and cephalexin. He was also allergic to bee stings. In addition he couldn't eat foods that contained sulfites, cinnamon, or MSG without experiencing adverse reactions."

At 6:10 I received a call from Bolen. "Good morning," Bolen said. "I've been going through John George's medical file and discovered he had allergies and sensitivities."

"That may be it!" I exclaimed. "If MSG is one of them you most likely have a case. You see, I know that my mother cannot eat anything with MSG without getting a terrific migraine. We always had to read ingredients carefully on any foods we purchased and we asked about foods at restaurants. I'm sure that Poor June had to know about John's MSG sensitivity, if he had one. Cooking for him would require knowing; therefore, all that Poor June had to do was buy some MSG or foods with MSG at the grocery store and ply John's breakfast food with it. It would have been one of the best-tasting breakfasts he ever had, because it tends to enhance the taste of food. It also would be sure to give him an unyielding migraine. That would have been the plan. One of them had previously made up the deadly capsules. I'm guessing Poor June did, because she had most likely saved oxycodone and fentanyl from her earlier surgeries. I don't know who purchased the heroin, but my guess would be the more obviously sleazy Robert Goodson made that deal. They surely thought they had the perfect plan. They nearly did. Actually, since they aren't arrested yet, maybe they did have the perfect plan."

"That is absolutely amazing, Harri," Bolen said. "What a revelation! I might even be able to use that information with my suspect this morning. Thank you, hugely! I owe you one." He paused. "I just had a thought, one really can't send flowers for thanks to a florist, can one? I know what it will be. Will you be home this evening?"

"I believe I should be," I answered. "My only plans right now are to take the girls for a walk."

"I'll give you a call later to see if it's all right to stop by," Bolen said, "if that works for you."

"Sure," I responded. "This should be interesting."

"Okay, then, I'm off to see a suspect," Bolen disclosed.

Before leaving his office, Bolen checked with the officer he had left in charge of the telephone records. He discovered that a text message had been sent to Glotz's personal cell phone and to the anonymous cell phone that could belong to Harper Rose Lewis. That text came from a different throwaway phone number; thus, it was fairly obvious that June had purchased a second disposable phone. The text was relatively clear. It said, "Caps considered. July." She was trying to let them know that the police had told her about the acetaminophen capsules. Doubtless she was also aware that she couldn't use her real name, but since the text was from a number her compatriots wouldn't recognize, she was trying to let them know it was from her while at the same time she was trying to throw the police off by using the name July instead of June. Not especially bright on her part. Also, if it was Harper who had the second phone, she may have already gotten rid of it and therefore would not be aware that June had been questioned.

Bolen headed out to find Harper Rose Lewis with the same two detectives who had been with him when they talked to June on Friday. They knew that she was expected at the courthouse by eight, and their plan was to catch her at home before she left for court. The plan worked. They discovered her just leaving home and heading toward her car when they arrived. Since she was already outside, Bolen asked her if she would talk to them in their car. She complied.

The first thing Bolen wanted to do was to get her fingerprints; thus he gave her a picture of Glotz to hold and asked her, "Do you know this man?"

She looked at the picture a long time as though trying to decide what answer she wanted to give. She finally said, "He looks familiar. I may have met him at some time."

Bolen took back the picture and placed it in an envelope and said. "We have some questions to ask you as a follow-up to John George's demise in the courthouse. We've been questioning all of the jurors and the people who worked at the courthouse a second time. We'll go to the station where we can be more comfortable. I'll have someone call your work for you to let them know that you will be a little late today." Harper Rose Lewis rode in silence to the police station.

After arriving and settling into a conference room, Bolen stated, "Ms Lewis, as an attorney, you know that you aren't in custody, that we haven't mirandized you and that you are free to leave at any time. Is that correct?"

"Yes," answered Ms Lewis

"However," Bolen continued, "here is what we know about the disposable telephone you had. You made a mistake in using it to call Maestro Alberto Morozov at the symphony office since it is the same phone that you used for keeping in touch with Herman Glotz, Robert Goodson and June George. We know you gave John George medication, as you were seen doing so. Yes, we know it came from an acetaminophen bottle. We also know that John had a migraine because his wife gave him MSG to bring it on. We know from emails and texts that we have obtained that there was a conspiracy between four of you to kill John George. We have the acetaminophen bottle that you threw away. It had your fingerprints on it. More importantly, an innocent homeless veteran discovered it and was killed by swallowing the capsules it contained. He only wanted to relieve the headache that was constantly with him after serving in the military in Afghanistan. Instead he died an agonizing death. We have your fingerprint also on the poker that killed Robert Goodson. What do you have to say?"

Obviously Bolen did not know all of the things he told Harper Rose Lewis that he knew. It was largely conjecture, but he wanted to come at her sounding strong, sounding sure in the knowledge that she was not only part of the conspiracy but also that she had murdered Robert Goodson and an innocent stranger. He was hopeful that what he claimed he knew would make her want to share with them anything that connected any of the four of them with this case or else prove to them that all the allegations were wrong. One or the other.

Harper Rose Lewis looked stunned, and then she asked, "You know all of that?"

Bolen answered, "Yes, we do. And even more."

"And you said a homeless man, a homeless veteran was killed by taking what he thought were acetaminophen capsules?" Ms Lewis asked.

"That's correct," Bolen answered and then thought to himself: "O, what a tangled web we weave when first we practice to deceive," as Sir Walter Scott once wrote.

"Oh no, Oh no," Ms Lewis said as she put her hands up on her head. She leaned down onto her lap and cried for several minutes. Then she grabbed a tissue from the box on the table, wiped her eyes and blew her nose and said, "Before my father committed suicide I overheard him talking to John George. I knew it was John George, because I had answered the phone and asked who was calling. I heard my dad ask him, no, plead with him, not to share what he knew about him. With his voice cracking my dad told John he couldn't bear it. It was only two hours after that phone call that my dad killed himself. I did not know what John George had against him, but I knew I wanted John George dead. He killed my father. I looked at it as justice. I still do. He was an evil man."

"June George contacted a few of the people who had been blackmailed by John to get together and talk about the situation," Harper Rose Lewis continued. "She included me, since she was aware of my father's suicide. We met a few times, and someone brought up murder. I had voiced that I would like to see John dead. Evidently he had caused June enormous problems in the years she had been married to him. Before long we decided that between us, as a group we would see that John ended up dead. We were just waiting for the perfect time, place, and means. We purchased disposable phones to keep in touch. During one of our meetings, Robert and Herman mentioned receiving a jury summons. About two weeks later June contacted us. She said John had also received a summons. She said she would let us know the date he was going to defer his jury duty to. She thought it was the opportune time and place, and she also had the method planned. My part was to do my best to get everyone onto the same jury; thus I had encouraged the bailiff to take the day off. I also made a point to go down to work with the courthouse employees to be sure I was able to get Robert, John, and Herman called and placed within the first twelve people in the line. The rest was up to them and the attorneys. Robert volunteered to get heroin to June, who had shared with us her plan for helping us rid the earth of John George. June had the rest of the medications and she put together the capsules."

"The plan worked exceedingly well because all three men were retained on the jury," Harper divulged, "and I was also available. June delivered the acetaminophen bottles to us the week before. Her other part of the plan was to fill John with MSG, since it always gave John a severe migraine, and she would hide his migraine medicine that morning. John loved to eat, so she knew he wouldn't pass up a great breakfast. I ran into John before court began. I asked him if he was all right. I told him he looked a little under the weather. He said he had the beginning of a migraine. I offered him acetaminophen, but he would take only one capsule. That one capsule by itself would not have been enough to do the job, because John dabbled in drugs upon occasion. When the migraine pain continued and John talked to Herman about it before the 10:30 court time, Herman was able to talk him into three or four capsules in hopes of lessening the pain from the migraine. Migraines can be terrible, so talking a migraine sufferer into taking several acetaminophen capsules was a no-brainer. Robert had made the offer, too, of his pills, so yes, we were all four in on John's death. I still don't consider it murder. To me, because of my father, it was definitely justice accomplished."

"However, it wasn't over yet." Harper went forward with her story. "Robert Goodson called me and requested that I come to his office. I went. He showed me what my father's file contained. He said he would give the information to the press unless I went along with his deal. He gave me my choice, I could give him eight hundred thousand dollars or myself for three months. I said no. I wouldn't do either. He walked to his desk and picked up the phone. He called the city newspaper and asked to speak to the editor. I couldn't have that happen. I couldn't have the information get out about my dad. I panicked, picked up the poker, and hit him and kept hitting him until he wasn't moving. I tried to wipe my prints off of the poker, but evidently I botched that job. Did I feel that killing Robert Goodson was justified? Yes and no. I cannot, however, justify at all that poor veteran who died because of my negligence. Because of that, let's just go ahead and I will give you my statement. As an attorney I know that none of the deaths were legally justified. It's almost mind boggling when I consider that I was instrumental in the death of three men."

Bolen then had the other two detectives take officers with them to go pick up Herman Glotz and June George, arrest them, and bring them in. He then headed into another room with Harper Rose Lewis. He set the room up for her to give a statement of evidence. She also told Bolen where her disposable phone could be located. She stated that she would be willing to testify in court; however, she wanted it made clear that her negligence alone was responsible for the death of the homeless veteran, not Herman's or June's.

Bolen told her that she needed to contact a lawyer and then he mirandized her. She told him that she did not need a lawyer. She also noted that she wouldn't expect any leniency for testifying, because she knew there could not be enough leniency to keep her from life in prison or maybe even the death penalty. She said, "I don't deserve leniency, anyway."

Before the court date, the fingerprints on the acetaminophen bottle and poker were proven to match the fingerprints of Harper Rose Lewis. There already was enough evidence to connect Herman Glotz for murder as well as blackmail and receiving union money. The police discovered June's second disposable phone. One other thing found during the search of her home was a capsule that had obviously fallen while June was making the drugs for John. It had rolled and had caught partially under the floor molding. It was an acetaminophen capsule and contained oxycodone, fentanyl and heroin. It was, as some say, the nail in the coffin.

Monday evening, around 7:30, Bolen called me and asked, "Is it still okay to come by?"

I stated that it was.

At 7:45, Bolen was at my door. As I opened it, I noticed a box in his hands. He handed it to me and said, "This is for you."

I took it and placed in on my dining room table. I opened it, and inside was an entire chocolate pie from Pie in the Sky. "Yes," I said, "this is better than getting me flowers, but you have to stay and have some with me. Will you?" I asked.

"I certainly will," Bolen responded. "I also thought we might have another one of these," he said.

I received another twenty-second kiss, which I must confess I did not mind in the least. "What am I going to do with you?" I asked after the kiss.

"I'm not sure," Bolen responded, "but I think we might need to figure that out."

I concurred. We just might need to figure that out.